PENGUIN BOOKS

THE DEATH OF GRASS

John Christopher was born in 1922 and educated at Peter Symonds School, Winchester. During the Second World War he served in the Royal Corps of Signals. He is a writer whose early interests were conditioned by pre-war American science fiction, and his own books such as *The Death of Grass* and *The World in Winter* have had that flavour, but the emphasis has been more on character than on scientific extrapolation. The writer of fiction he most admires is Jane Austen. He writes (under an assumed name) general novels to which critics and public alike display a massive indifference, but his books for children such as *The White Mountain*, *The City of Gold and Lead*, *The Pool of Fire* and *The Lotus Caves* have enjoyed considerable success. His latest novel is *Pendulum*.

John Christopher, who was born at Knowsley in Lancashire, was involuntarily transported at the age of ten to Hampshire, a manoeuvre which he regards as in a sense equivalent to Dickens's banishment to the blacking factory. He is now, however, so reconciled to the South that he has settled with his wife and children on the island of Guernsey.

[illegible]

[illegible]

[illegible] was born in [illegible] [illegible]

[illegible]

JOHN CHRISTOPHER

THE DEATH OF GRASS

*

PENGUIN BOOKS

Penguin Books Ltd, Harmondsworth, Middlesex, England
Penguin Books Australia Ltd, Ringwood, Victoria, Australia

—

First published by Michael Joseph 1956
Published in Penguin Books 1958
Reprinted 1963, 1970

Made and printed in Great Britain
by Hunt Barnard Printing Ltd,
Aylesbury

PRODROME

As sometimes happens, death healed a family breach.

When Hilda Custance was widowed in the early summer of 1933, she wrote, for the first time since her marriage thirteen years before, to her father. Their moods touched – hers of longing for the hills of Westmorland after the grim seasons of London, and his of loneliness and the desire to see his only daughter again, and his unknown grandsons, before he died. The boys, who were away at school, had not been brought back for the funeral, and at the end of the summer term they returned to the small house at Richmond only for a night, before, with their mother, they travelled north.

In the train, John, the younger boy, said:

'But *why* did we never have anything to do with Grandfather Beverley?'

His mother looked out of the window at the tarnished grimy environs of London, wavering, as though with fatigue, in the heat of the day.

She said vaguely: 'It's hard to know how these things happen. Quarrels begin, and neither person stops them, and they become silences, and nobody breaks them.'

She thought calmly of the storm of emotions into which she had plunged, out of the untroubled quiet life of her girlhood in the valley. She had been sure that, whatever unhappiness came after, she would never regret the passion itself. Time had proved her doubly wrong; first in the contentment of her married life and her children, and later in the amazement that such contentment could have come out of what she saw, in retrospect, as squalid and ill-directed. She had not seen the squalidness of it then, but her father could hardly fail to be aware of it, and had not been able to conceal his awareness. That had been the key: his disgust and her resentment.

John asked her: 'But who started the quarrel?'

She was only sorry that it had meant that the two men never

knew each other. They were not unlike in many ways, and she thought they would have liked each other if her pride had not prevented it.

'It doesn't matter,' she said, 'now.'

David put down his copy of the *Boy's Own Paper*. Although a year older than his brother, he was only fractionally taller; they had a strong physical resemblance and were often taken for twins. But David was slower moving and slower in thought than John, and fonder of things than of ideas.

He said: 'The valley – what's it like, Mummy?'

'The valley? Wonderful. It's . . . No, I think it will be better if it comes as a surprise to you. I couldn't describe it anyway.'

John said: 'Oh, do, Mummy!'

David asked thoughtfully: 'Shall we see it from the train?'

Their mother laughed. 'From the train? Not even the beginnings of it. It's nearly an hour's run from Stavely.'

'How big is it?' John asked. 'Are there hills all round?'

She smiled at them. 'You'll see.'

Jess Hillen, their grandfather's tenant farmer, met them with a car at Stavely, and they drove up into the hills. The day was nearly spent, and they saw Blind Gill at last with the sun setting behind them.

Cyclops Valley would have been a better name for it for it looked out of one eye only – towards the west. But for this break, it was like a saucer, or a deep dish, the sides sloping up – bare rock or rough heather – to the overlooking sky. Against that enclosing barrenness, the valley's richness was the more marked; green wheat swayed inwards with the summer breeze, and beyond the wheat, as the ground rose, they saw the lusher green of pasture.

The entrance to the valley could scarcely have been narrower. To the left of the road, ten yards away, a rock face rose sharply and overhung. To the right, the River Lepe foamed against the road's very edge. Its further bank, fifteen yards beyond, hugged the other jaw of the valley.

Hilda Custance turned round to look at her sons.

'Well?'

'Gosh!' John said, 'this river ... I mean – how does it get into the valley in the first place?'

'It's the Lepe. Thirty-five miles long, and twenty-five of those miles underground, if the stories are to be believed. Anyway, it comes from underground in the valley. There are a lot of rivers like that in these parts.'

'It looks deep.'

'It is. And very fast. No bathing, I'm afraid. It's wired farther up to keep cattle out. They don't stand a chance if they fall in.'

John remarked sagely: 'I should think it might flood in winter.'

His mother nodded. 'It always used to. Does it still, Jess?'

'Cut off a month last winter,' Jess said. 'It's not so bad now we have the wireless.'

'I think it's terrific,' John said. 'But are you really cut off? You could climb the hills.'

Jess grinned. 'There are some who have. But it's a rocky road up, and rockier still down the other side. Best to sit tight when the Lepe runs full.'

Hilda Custance looked at her elder son. He was staring ahead at the valley, thickly shadowed by sunset; the buildings of the Hillen farm were in view now, but not the Beverley farm high up.

'Well,' she said, 'what do you think of it, David?'

Reluctantly he turned his gaze inwards to meet her own. He said: 'I think I'd like to live here, always.'

That summer, the boys ran wild in the valley.

It was some three miles long, and perhaps half a mile wide at its greatest extent. It held only the two farms, and the river, which issued from the southern face about two miles in. The ground was rich and well cropped, but there was plenty of room for boys of twelve and eleven to play, and there were the surrounding hills to climb.

They made the ascent at two or three points, and stood, panting, looking out over rough hills and moorlands. The valley was tiny behind them. John delighted in the feeling of height, of isolation, and, to some extent, of power; for the farm-houses looked, from this vantage, like toy buildings that they might reach down and pluck from the ground. And in its greenness the valley seemed an oasis among desert mountains.

David took less pleasure in this, and after their third climb he refused to go again. It was enough for him to be in the valley; the surrounding slopes were like cupped and guarding hands, which it was both fruitless and ungrateful to scale.

This divergence of their interests caused them to spend much of their time apart. While John roamed the valley's sides, David kept to the farmland, to his grandfather's increasing satisfaction. At the end of the second week, boy and old man, they went together to the River field on a warm and cloudy afternoon. The boy watched intently while his grandfather plucked ears of wheat here and there, and examined them. His near vision was poor, and he was forced to hold the wheat at arm's length.

'It's going to be a fair crop,' he said, 'as well as my eyes can tell me.'

To their right there was the continuous dull roar as the Lepe forced its way out of the containing rock into the valley.

David said: 'Shall we still be here for the harvest?'

'Depends. It may be. Would you like to be?'

David said enthusiastically: 'Oh, yes, Grandfather!'

There was a silence in which the only intrusion was the noise of the Lepe. His grandfather looked over the valley which the Beverley's had farmed for a century and a half; and then turned from the land to the boy at his side.

'I don't see as we shall have long to get to know one another, David boy,' he said. 'Do you think you would like to farm this valley when you're grown?'

'More than anything.'

'It'll be yours, then. A farm needs one owner, and I don't think as your brother would be fond of the life, any road.'

'John wants to be an engineer,' David said.

'And he'll be likely enough to make a good one. What had you thought of being, then?'

'I hadn't thought of anything.'

'I shouldn't say it, maybe,' said his grandfather, 'since I've never seen ought of any other kind of life but what I glimpse at Lepeton Market; but I don't know of another life that can give as much satisfaction. And this is good land, and a good lie for a man that's content with his own company and few neighbours. There's stone slabs under the ground in the Top Meadow, and they say the valley was held as a stronghold once, in bygone times. I don't reckon you could hold it now, against guns and aeroplanes, but whenever I've been outside I've always had a feeling that I could shut the door behind me when I come back through the pass.'

'I felt that,' David said, 'when we came in.'

'My grandfather,' said David's grandfather, 'had himself buried here. They didn't like it even then, but in those days they had to put up with some things they didn't like. They've got more weight behind them today, damn them! A man should have the rights to be buried in his own ground.'

He looked across the green spears of wheat.

'But I shan't fret so greatly over leaving it, if I'm leaving it to my own blood.'

On another afternoon, John stood on the southern rim and, after staring his fill, began to descend again into the valley.

The Lepe, from its emergence to the point where it left the valley altogether, hugged these southern slopes, and for that reason they could only be scaled from the eastern end of the valley. But the boy realized now that, once above the river, it could not bar him from the slopes beneath which it raced and boiled. From the ground, he had seen a cleft in the hill face which might be a cave. He climbed down towards it, breaking new ground.

He worked his way down with agility but with care, for although quick in thought and movement he was not foolhardy. He came at last to the cleft, perhaps fifteen feet above the dark swirling waters, and found it to be no more than that. In his disappointment, he looked for some new target of ambition. Directly over the river's edge, rock swelled into something like a ledge. From there, perhaps, one could dangle one's legs in the rushing water. It was less than a cave would have been, but better than a return, baulked of any satisfaction, to the farmland.

He lowered himself still more cautiously. The slope was steep, and the sound of the Lepe had a threatening growl to it. The ledge, when he finally reached it, gave little purchase.

By now, however, the idea had come to obsess him – just one foot in the water; that would be enough to meet the objective he had set himself. Pressed awkwardly against the side of the hill, he reached down with his hand to unfasten the sandal on his right foot. As he did so, his left foot slipped on the smooth rock. He clutched frantically, aware of himself falling, but there was no hold for his hands. He fell and the waters of the Lepe – chill even in midsummer, and savagely buffeting – took him.

He could swim fairly well for a boy of his age, but he had no chance against the violence of the Lepe. The current pulled him down into the deeps of the channel that the river had worn for itself through centuries before the Beverleys, or any others, had come to farm its banks. It rolled him like a pebble along its bed, as though to squeeze breath and life from him together. He was aware of nothing but its all-embracing violence and his own choking pulse.

Then, suddenly, he saw that the darkness about him was diminishing, yielding to sunlight filtered through water still violent but of no great depth. With his last strength, he struggled into an upright position, and his head broke through to the air. He took shuddering breath, and saw that he was near the middle of the river. He could not stand, for the river's strength was too great, but he half-ran, half-swam with the current as the Lepe dragged him towards the pass that marked the valley's end.

Once out of the valley, the river took a quieter course. A hundred yards down, he was able to swim awkwardly, through relatively calm water, to the farther bank, and pull himself up on to it. Drenched and exhausted, he contemplated the length of the tumbling flood down which, in so short a time, he had been carried. He was still staring when he heard the sound of a pony-trap coming up the road and, a few moments later, his grandfather's voice.

'Hey, there, John! Been swimming?'

He got to his feet unsteadily, and stumbled towards the trap. His grandfather's arms took him and lifted him.

'You've had a bit of a shaking, lad. Did you fall in then?'

His mind remained shocked; he told as much as he could, flat-voiced, in broken sentences. The old man listened.

'It looks like you were born for a hanging. A grown man wouldn't give overmuch for his chances if he'd gone in like that. And you broke surface with your feet still on the bottom, you say? My father used to tell of a bar in the middle of the Lepe, but nobody was like to try it. It's deep enough by either bank.'

He looked at the boy, who had begun to shiver, more from the aftermath of his experience than from anything else.

'No sense in me going on talking all afternoon, though. We must get you back, and into dry clothes. Come on there, Flossie!'

As his grandfather cracked the small whip, John said quickly: 'Grandfather – you won't say anything to Mummy, will you? Please!'

The old man said: 'How shall we not, then? She can't but see you're soaked to the bone.'

'I thought I might dry myself ... in the sun.'

'Ay, but not this week! Still ... you don't want her to know you've had a ducking? Are you feared she'll scold you?'

'No.'

Their eyes met. 'Ah, well,' said his grandfather, 'I reckon I owe you a secret, lad. Will it do if I take you to the Hillens and get you dried there? You shall have to be dried somewhere.'

'Yes,' John said, 'I don't mind that. Thank you, Grandfather.'

The wheels of the trap crunched over the rough stone road as they passed through the gap and the Hillen farm came into view ahead of them. The old man broke the silence between them.

'You want to be an engineer, then?'

John looked away from his fascinated watching of the rushing Lepe. 'Yes, Grandfather.'

'You wouldn't take to farming?'

John said cautiously: 'Not particularly.'

His grandfather said, with relief: 'No, I thought not.'

He began to say more, but broke off. It was not until they were within hail of the Hillen farm buildings that he said:

'I'm glad of it. I love the land more than most, I reckon, but there are some terms on which it isn't worth having. The best land in the world might as well be barren if it brings bad blood between brothers.'

Then he reined up the pony, and called out to Jess Hillen.

ONE

A QUARTER of a century later, the two brothers stood together by the banks of the Lepe. David lifted his stick and pointed far up the slope of the hill.

'There they go!'

John followed his brother's gaze to where the two specks toiled their way upwards. He laughed.

'Davey setting the pace as usual, but I would put my money on Mary's stamina for first-over-the-top.'

'She's a couple of years older, remember.'

'You're a bad uncle. You favour the nephew too blatantly.'

They both grinned. 'She's a good girl,' David said, 'but Davey – well, he's Davey.'

'You should have married and got a few of your own.'

'I never had the time to go courting.'

John said: 'I thought you countrymen took that in your stride, along with the cabbage planting.'

'I don't plant cabbages, though. There's no sense in doing anything but wheat and potatoes these days. That's what the Government wants, so that's what I give 'em.'

John looked at him with amusement. 'I like you in your part of the honest, awkward farmer. What about your beef cattle, though? And the dairy herd?'

'I was talking about crops. I think the dairy cattle will have to go, anyway. They take up more land than they're worth.'

John shook his head. 'I can't imagine the valley without cows.'

'The townie's old illusion,' David said, 'of the unchanging countryside. The country changes more than the city does. With the city it's only a matter of different buildings – bigger maybe, and uglier, but no more than that. When the country changes, it changes in a more fundamental way altogether.'

'We could argue about that,' John said. 'After all ... '

David looked over his shoulder. 'Here's Ann coming.' When she was in earshot, he added: 'And you ask me why I never got married!'

Ann put an arm on each of their shoulders. 'What I like about the valley,' she said, 'is the high standard of courtly compliments. Do you really want to know why you never married, David?'

'He tells me he's never had the time,' John said.

'You're a hybrid,' Ann told him. 'You're enough of a farmer to know that a wife should be a chattel, but being one of the new-fangled university-trained kind, you have the grace to feel guilty about it.'

'And how do you reckon I would treat my wife,' David asked, 'assuming I brought myself to the point of getting one? Yoke her up to the plough when the tractor broke down?'

'It would depend on the wife, I should think – on whether she was able to master you or not.'

'She might yoke you to the plough!' John commented.

'You will have to find me a nice masterful one, Ann. Surely you've got some women friends who could cope with a Westmorland clod?'

'I've been discouraged,' Ann said. 'Look how hard I used to try, and it never got anywhere.'

'Now, then! They were all either flat-chested and bespectacled, with dirty fingers and a *New Statesman* tucked behind their left ear; or else dressed in funny-coloured tweeds, nylons, and high-heeled shoes.'

'What about Norma?'

'Norma,' David said, 'wanted to see the stallion servicing one of the mares. She thought it would be a highly interesting experience.'

'Well, what's wrong with that in a farmer's wife?'

David said drily: 'I've no idea. But it shocked old Jess when he heard her. We have our rough-and-ready notions of decorum, funny though they may be.'

'It's just as I said,' Ann told him. 'You're still partly civilized. You'll be a bachelor all your days.'

David grinned. 'What I want to know is – am I going to get Davey to reduce to my own condition of barbarism?'

John said: 'Davey is going to be an architect. I want to have some sensible plans to work to in my old age. You should see the monstrosity I'm helping to put up now.'

'Davey will do as he wishes,' Ann said. 'I think his present notion is that he's going to be a mountaineer. What about Mary? Aren't you going to fight over her?'

'I don't see Mary as an architect,' her father said.

'Mary will marry,' her uncle added, 'like any woman who's worth anything.'

Ann contemplated them. 'You're both savages really,' she observed. 'I suppose all men are. It's just that David's had more of his veneer of civilization chipped off.'

'Now,' David said, 'what's wrong with taking it for granted that a good woman will marry?'

'I wouldn't be surprised if Davey marries, too,' Ann said.

'There was a girl in my year at the university,' David said. 'She had every one of us beat for theory, and from what I heard she'd been more or less running her father's farm in Lancashire since she was about fourteen. She didn't even take her degree. She married an American airman and went back with him to live in Detroit.'

'And therefore,' Ann observed, 'take no thought for your daughters, who will inevitably marry American airmen and go and live in Detroit.'

David smiled slowly. 'Well, something like that!'

Ann threw him a look half-tolerant, half-exasperated, but made no further comment. They walked together in silence by the river bank. The air had the lift of May; the sky was blue and white, with clouds browsing slowly across their azure pasture. In the valley, one was always more conscious of the sky, framed as it was by the encircling hills. A shadow sailed across the ground towards them, enveloped them, and yielded again to sunshine.

'This peaceful land,' Ann said. 'You are lucky, David.'

'Don't go back on Sunday,' he suggested. 'Stay here. We could do with some extra hands for the potatoes with Luke away sick.'

'My monstrosity calls me,' John said. 'And the kids will never do their holiday tasks while they stay here. I'm afraid it's back to London on schedule.'

'There's such a richness everywhere. Look at all this, and then think of the poor wretched Chinese.'

'What's the latest? Did you hear the news before you came out?'

'The Americans are sending more grain ships.'

'Anything from Peking?'

'Nothing official. It's supposed to be in flames. And at Hong Kong they've had to repel attacks across the frontier.'

'A genteel way of putting it,' John said grimly. 'Did you ever see those old pictures of the rabbit plagues in Australia? Wire-netting fences ten feet high, and rabbits – hundreds, thousands of rabbits – piled up against them, leap-frogging over each other until in the end either they scaled the fences or the fences went down under their weight. That's Hong Kong right now, except that it's not rabbits piled against the fence but human beings.'

'Do you think it's as bad as that?' David asked.

'Worse, if anything. The rabbits only advanced under the blind instinct of hunger. Men are intelligent, and because they're intelligent you have to take sterner measures to stop them. I suppose they've got plenty of ammunition for their guns, but it's certain they won't have enough.'

'You think Hong Kong will fall?'

'I'm sure it will. The pressure will build up until it has to. They may machine-gun them from the air first, and dive-bomb them and drop napalm on them, but for every one they kill there will be a hundred trekking in from the interior to replace him.'

'Napalm!' Ann said. 'Oh, no.'

'What else? It's that or evacuate, and there aren't the ships to evacuate the whole of Hong Kong in time.'

David said: 'But if they took Hong Kong – there can't be enough food there to give them three square meals, and then they're back where they started.'

'Three square meals? Not even one, I shouldn't think. But what difference does that make? Those people are starving. When you're in that condition, it's the next mouthful that you're willing to commit murder for.'

'And India?' David asked. 'And Burma, and all the rest of Asia?'

'God knows. At least, they've got some warning. It was the Chinese government's unwillingness to admit they were faced with a problem they couldn't master that's got them in the worst of this mess.'

Ann said: 'How did they possibly imagine they could keep it a secret?'

John shrugged. 'They had abolished famine by statute – remember? And then, things looked easy at the beginning. They isolated the virus within a month of it hitting the rice-fields. They had it neatly labelled – the Chung-Li virus. All they had to do was to find a way of killing it which didn't kill the plant. Alternatively, they could breed a virus-resistant strain. And finally, they had no reason to expect the virus would spread so fast.'

'But when the crop had failed so badly?'

'They'd built up stocks against famine – give them credit for that. They thought they could last out until the spring crops were cut. And they couldn't believe they wouldn't have beaten the virus by then.'

'The American's think they've got an angle on it.'

'They may save the rest of the Far East. They're too late to save China – and that means Hong Kong.'

Ann's eyes were on the hillside, and the two figures clambering up to the summit.

'Little children starving,' she said. 'Surely there's something we can do about it?'

'What?' John asked. 'We're sending food, but it's a drop in the ocean.'

'And we can talk and laugh and joke,' she said, 'in a land as peaceful and rich as this, while *that* goes on.'

David said: 'Not much else we can do, is there, my dear? There were enough people dying in agony every minute before; all this does is multiply it. Death's the same, whether it's happening to one or a hundred thousand.'

She said; 'I suppose it is.'

'We've been lucky,' David said. 'A virus could have hit wheat in just the same way.'

'It wouldn't have had the same effect, though, would it?' John asked. 'We don't depend on wheat in quite the way the Chinese, and Asiatics generally, depend on rice.'

'Bad enough, though. Rationed bread, for a certainty.'

'Rationed bread!' Ann exclaimed. 'And in China there are millions fighting for a mouthful of grain.'

They were silent. Above them, the sun stood in a sector of cloudless sky. The song of a mistle-thrush lifted above the steady comforting undertone of the Lepe.

'Poor devils,' David said.

'Coming up in the train,' John observed, 'there was a man who was explaining, with evident delight, that the Chinks were getting what they deserved for being Communists. But for the presence of the children, I think I would have given him the benefit of my opinion of him.'

'Are we very much better?' Ann asked. 'We remember and feel sorry now and then, but the rest of the time we forget, and go about our business as usual.'

'We have to,' David said. 'The fellow in the train – I shouldn't think he gloats all the time. It's the way we're made. It's not so bad as long as we realize how lucky we are.'

'Isn't it? Didn't Dives say something like that?'

They heard, carried on the breeze of early summer, a faint hallooing, and their eyes went up to it. A figure stood outlined against the sky and, as they watched, another clambered up to stand beside it.

John smiled. 'Mary first. Stamina told.'

'You mean, age did,' David said. 'Let's give them a wave to show we've seen 'em.'

They waved their arms, and the two specks waved back to them. When they resumed their walk, Ann said:

'As a matter of fact, I think Mary's decided she's going to be a doctor.'

'Now, that's a sensible idea,' David said. 'She can always marry another doctor, and set up a joint practice.'

'What,' John said, ' – in Detroit?'

'It's one of the useful arts as David sees them,' Ann remarked. 'On a par with being a good cook.'

David poked into a hole with his stick. 'Living closer to the simple things as I do,' he said, 'I have a better appreciation of them. I put the useful arts first, second, and third. After that it's all right to start messing about with sky-scrapers.'

'Now,' John said, 'if you hadn't had engineers to build a contraption big enough to fit the Ministry of Agriculture into, where would all you farmers be?'

David did not reply to the jest. Their walk had taken them to a place where, with the river on their left, the path was flanked to the right by swampy ground. David bent down towards a clump of grass, whose culms rose some two feet high. He gave a tug, and two or three stems came out easily.

'Noxious weeds?' Ann asked.

David shook his head. '*Oryzoides,* of the genus *Leersia,* of the tribe *Oryzae.*'

'Without your botanical background,' John said, 'it just doesn't mean a thing.'

'It's an uncommon British grass,' David went on. 'Very uncommon in these parts – you find it occasionally in the southern counties – Hampshire, Surrey, and so on.'

'The leaves,' Ann said, ' – they look as though they're rotting.'

'So are the roots,' David said. '*Oryzae* includes three genera. *Leersia* is one and *Oryza*'s another.'

'They sound like names of progressive females,' John commented.

'*Oryza sativa,*' David said, 'is rice.'

'Rice!' said Ann. 'Then ... '

'This is rice grass,' David said. He pulled a long blade and held it up. It was speckled with patches of darker green centred with brown; the last inch was all brown and deliquescing. 'And this is the Chung-Li virus.'

'Here,' John asked, 'in England?'

'In this green and pleasant land,' David said. 'I knew it went for *Leersia* as well, but I hadn't expected it to reach so far.'

Ann stared in fascination at the splotched and putrefying grass. 'This,' she said. 'Just this.'

David looked across the stretch of marsh to the cornfield beyond.

'Thank God that viruses have selective appetites. That damn thing comes half-way across the world to fasten on this one small clump of grass – perhaps on a few hundred clumps like it in all England.'

'Yes,' John said, 'wheat is a grass too, isn't it?'

'Wheat,' David said, 'and oats and barley and rye – not to mention fodder for the beasts. It's rough on the Chinese, but it could have been a lot worse.'

'Yes,' Ann said, 'it could have been us instead. Isn't that what you mean? We had forgotten them again. And probably in another five minutes we shall have found some other excuse for forgetting them.'

David crumpled the grass in his hand, and threw it into the river. It sped away on the swiftly flowing Lepe.

'Nothing else we can do,' he said.

TWO

ANN, who was dummy, switched the wireless on for the nine o'clock news. John had landed in a three no-trumps contract which they could not possibly make, chiefly to shut out Roger and Olivia, who only wanted thirty for game and rubber. John frowned over his cards.

Roger Buckley said boisterously: 'Come on, old boy! What about finessing that nine?'

Roger was the only one of John's old Army friends with whom he had kept in close touch. Ann had not cared for him on first acquaintance, and longer experience had not moved her towards anything more than tolerance. She disliked his general air of schoolboyish high spirits almost as much as his rarer moments of savage depression, and she disliked still more what she saw as the essential hardness that stood behind both aspects of his outward personality.

She was reasonably sure that he knew what her feelings were, and discounted them – as he did so many things – as unimportant. In the past, this had added further to her dislike, and but for one thing she would have weaned John away from the friendship.

The one thing was Olivia. When Roger, fairly soon after her first meeting with him, had brought along this rather large, placid, shy girl, introducing her as his fiancée, Ann had been surprised, but confident that this engagement – the latest of several by John's report – would never end in marriage. She had been wrong in that. She had befriended Olivia in the first place in anticipation that Roger would leave her stranded, and subsequently so that she could be in a position to protect her when, after marriage, Roger showed his true colours. She had been humiliated to find, by degrees, not only that Olivia continued to enjoy what seemed to be an entirely happy marriage, but also that she herself had come to depend a great deal on Olivia's warm quiet understanding in her own minor crises. Without liking

Roger any more, she was more willing to put up with him on account of Olivia.

John led a small diamond towards King – Jack in dummy. Olivia placidly set down an eight. John hesitated, and then brought down the Jack. With a triumphant chuckle, Roger dropped the Queen on top of it.

From the radio, a voice said, in B.B.C. accents:

'The United Nations Emergency Committee on China, in its interim report published today, has stated that the lowest possible figure for deaths in the China famine must be set at two hundred million people . . . '

Roger said: 'Dummy looks a bit weak in hearts. I think we might try them out.'

Ann said: 'Two hundred million! It's unbelievable.'

'What's two hundred million?' Roger asked. 'There's an awful lot of Chinks in China. They'll breed 'em back again in a couple of generations.'

Ann had encountered Roger's cynicism in argument before, and preferred not to do so at this moment. Her mind was engaged with the horrors of her own imagination.

'A further item of the report,' the announcer's voice continued, 'reveals that field tests with Isotope 717 have shown an almost complete control of the Chung-Li virus. The spraying of all rice fields with this isotope is to be carried out as an urgent operation by the newly constituted United Nations Air Relief Wing. Supplies of the isotope are expected to be adequate to cover all the rice fields immediately threatened within a few days, and the remainder within a month.'

'Thank God for that,' John said.

'When you've finished the Magnificat,' Roger said, 'you might cover that little heart.'

In mild protest, Olivia said: 'Roger!'

'Two hundred million,' John said. 'A sizeable monument to human pride and stubbornness. If they'd let our people work on the virus six months earlier they would have been alive now.'

'Talking of sizeable monuments to human pride,' Roger said, 'and since you insist on stalling before you bring that Ace of hearts out, how's your own little Taj Mahal going? I hear rumours of labour troubles.'

'Is there anything you don't hear?'

Roger was Public Relations Officer to the Ministry of Production. He lived in a world of gossip and whitewash that fostered, Ann thought, his natural inhumanity.

'Nothing of importance,' Roger said. 'Do you think you'll get it finished on time?'

'Tell your Minister,' John said, 'to tell his colleague that he need have no fears. His plush-lined suite will be ready for him right on the dot.'

'The question,' Roger commented, 'is whether the colleague will be ready for it.'

'Another rumour?'

'I wouldn't call it a rumour. Of course, he might turn out to have an axe-proof neck. It will be interesting to see.'

'Roger,' Ann asked, 'do you get a great deal of pleasure out of the contemplation of human misfortune?'

She was sorry, as soon as she had said it, that she had let herself be provoked into reacting. Roger fixed her with an amused eye; he had a deceptively mild face with a chin that, from some angles, appeared to recede, and large brown eyes.

'I'm the little boy who never grew up,' he said. 'When you were my age, you probably laughed too at fat men sliding on banana skins. Now you think of them breaking their necks and leaving behind despairing wives and a horde of under-nourished children. You must let me go on enjoying my toys as best I can.'

Olivia said: 'He's hopeless. You mustn't mind him, Ann.'

She spoke with the amused tolerance an indulgent mother might show towards a naughty child. But what was suitable in relation to a child, Ann thought with irritation, was not therefore to be regarded as an adequate way of dealing with a morally backward adult.

Still watching Ann, Roger continued: 'The thing all you adult, sensitive people must bear in mind is that things are on your side at present – you live in a world where everything's in favour of being sensitive and civilized. But it's a precarious business. Look at the years China's been civilized, and look what's just happened out there. When the belly starts rumbling, the belly-laugh comes into its own again.'

'I'm inclined to agree,' John said. 'You're a throwback, Roger.'

'There are some ways,' Olivia said, 'in which he and Steve are just about the same age.'

Steve was the Buckleys' nine-year-old son; Roger was too devoted to him to let him go away to school. He was rather small, decidedly precocious, and capable of bouts of elemental savagery.

'But Steve will grow out of it,' Ann pointed out.

Roger grinned. 'If he does, he's no son of mine!'

The children came home for half-term, and the Custances and the Buckleys drove down to the sea for the week-end. It was their custom to hire a caravan between them; the caravan, towed down by one car and back by the other, housed the four adults, while the three children slept in a tent close by.

They had good weather for the trip, and Saturday morning found them lying on sun-warmed shingle, within sound and sight of the sea. The children interspersed this with bathing or with crab-hunting along the shore. Of the adults, John and the two women were happy enough to lie in the sun. Roger, more restless by nature, first assisted the children and then lay about in evident and increasing frustration.

When Roger had looked at his watch several times, John said: 'All right. Let's go and get changed.'

'All right, what?' Ann asked. 'What are you getting changed for? You weren't proposing to do the cooking, were you?'

'Roger's been tripping over his tongue for the last half-hour,' John said. 'I think I'd better take him for a run down to the village. They'll be open by now.'

'They were open half an hour ago,' Roger said. 'We'll take your car.'

'Lunch at one,' Olivia said. 'And not kept for latecomers.'

'Don't worry.'

With glasses in front of them, Roger said:

'That's better. The seaside always makes me thirsty. Must be the salt in the air.'

John drank from his glass, and put it down again.

'You're a bit jumpy, Rodge. I noticed it yesterday. Something bothering you?'

They sat in the bar parlour. The door was open, and they could look out on to a gravelled patch on this side of the road, and a wide stretch of green beyond it. The air was warm and mild.

'This is the weather the cuckoo likes,' Roger quoted. 'When they sit outside the "Traveller's Rest," and maids come forth sprig-muslin drest, and citizens dream of the South and West. And so do I. Jumpy? Perhaps I am.'

'Anything I can lend a hand with?'

Roger studied him for a moment. 'The first duty of a Public Relations Officer,' he said, 'is loyalty, the second is discretion, and having a loud mouth with a ready tongue runs a poor third. My trouble is that I always keep my fingers crossed when I pledge loyalty and discretion to anyone who isn't a personal friend.'

'What's up?'

'If you were me,' Roger said, 'you wouldn't tell, honesty being one of your stumbling-blocks. So I can tell you to keep it under your hat. Not even Ann yet. I haven't said anything to Olivia.'

'If it's that important,' John said, 'perhaps you'd better not say anything to me.'

'Frankly, I think they would have been wiser not to keep it dark, but that's not the point either. All I'm concerned with is that nothing that gets out can be traced back to me. It will get out – that's certain.'

'Now I'm curious,' John said.

Roger emptied his glass, waited for John to do the same, and took them both over to the bar for refilling. When he had brought them back, he drank lengthily before saying anything further.

He said: 'Remember Isotope 717?'

'The stuff they sprayed the rice with?'

'Yes. There were two schools of thought about tackling that virus. One wanted to find something that would kill the virus; the other thought the best line was breeding a virus-resistant rice strain. The second obviously required more time, and so got less attention. Then the people on the first tack came up with

717, found it overwhelmingly effective against the virus, and rushed it into action.'

'It did kill the virus,' John said. 'I've seen the pictures of it.'

'From what I've heard, viruses are funny brutes. Now, if they'd found a virus-resistant rice, that would have solved the problem properly. You can almost certainly find a resistant strain of anything, if you look hard enough or work on a large enough scale.'

John looked at him. 'Go on.'

'Apparently, it was a complex virus. They've identified at least five phases by now. When they came up with 717 they had found four phases, and 717 killed them all. They discovered number five when they found they hadn't wiped the virus out after all.'

'But in that case ...'

'Chung-Li,' said Roger, 'is well ahead on points.'

John said: 'You mean, there's still a trace of the virus active in the fields? It can't be more than a trace, considering how effective 717 was.'

'Only a trace,' Roger said. 'Of course, we might have been lucky. Phase 5 might have been slow where the other four were fast movers. From what I hear, though, it spreads quite as fast as the original.'

John said slowly: 'So we're back where we started. Or not quite where we started. After all, if they found something to cope with the first four phases they should be able to lick the fifth.'

'That's what I tell myself,' Roger said. 'There's just the other thing that's unsettling.'

'Well?'

'Phase 5 was masked by the others before 717 got to work. I don't know how this business applies, but the stronger virus strains somehow kept it inactive. When 717 removed them, it was able to go ahead and show its teeth. It differs from its big brothers in one important respect.'

John waited; Roger took a draught of beer.

Roger went on: 'The appetite of the Chung-Li virus was for the tribe of *Oryzae*, of the family of *Gramineae*. Phase 5 is rather less discriminating. It thrives on all the *Gramineae*.'

'*Gramineae!*'

Roger smiled, not very happily. 'I've only picked up the jargon recently myself. *Gramineae* means grasses – all the grasses.'

John thought of David. "We've been lucky." 'Grasses,' he said, ' – that includes wheat.'

'Wheat, oats, barley, rye – that's a starter. Then meat, dairy foods, poultry. In a couple of years' time we'll be living on fish and chips – if we can get the fat to fry them in.'

'They'll find an answer to it.'

'Yes,' Roger said, 'of course they will. They found an answer to the original virus, didn't they? I wonder in what directions Phase 6 will extend its range – to potatoes, maybe?'

John had a thought. 'If they're keeping it quiet – I take it this is on an international level – might it not be because they're reasonably sure an answer is already in the bag?'

'That's one way of looking at it. My own feeling was that they might be waiting until they have got the machine-guns into position.'

'Machine-guns?'

'They've got to be ready,' Roger said, 'for the second two hundred million.'

'It can't come to that. Not with all the world's resources working on it right from the beginning. After all, if the Chinese had had the sense to call in help ...'

'We're a brilliant race,' Roger observed. 'We found out how to use coal and oil, and when they showed the first signs of running out we got ready to hop on the nuclear energy wagon. The mind boggles at man's progress in the last hundred years. If I were a Martian, I wouldn't take odds even of a thousand to one on intellect of that kind being defeated by a little thing like a virus. Don't think I'm not an optimist, but I like to hedge my bets even when the odds look good.'

'Even if you look at it from the worst point of view,' John said, 'we probably could live on fish and vegetables. It wouldn't be the end of the world.'

'Could we?' Roger asked. 'All of us? Not on our present amount of food intake.'

'One picks up some useful information from having a farmer in the family,' John said. 'An acre of land yields between one and two hundredweight of meat, or thirty hundredweight of bread. But it will yield ten tons of potatoes.'

'You encourage me,' Roger commented. 'I am now prepared to believe that Phase 5 will not wipe out the human race. That leaves me only my own immediate circle to worry about. I can disengage my attention from the major issues.'

'Damn it!' John said. 'This isn't China.'

'No,' Roger said. 'This is a country of fifty million people that imports nearly half its food requirements.'

'We may have to tighten our belts.'

'A tight belt,' said Roger, 'looks silly on a skeleton.'

'I've told you,' John said, ' – if you plant potatoes instead of grain crops you get a bulk yield that's more than six times heavier.'

'Now go and tell the government. On second thoughts, don't. Whatever the prospects, I'm not prepared to throw my job in. And there, unless I'm a long way off the mark, you have the essential clue. Even if I thought you were the only man who had that information, and thought that information might save us all from starvation, I should think twice before I advised you to advertise my own security failings.'

'Twice, possibly,' John said, 'but not three times. It would be your future as well.'

'Ah,' said Roger, 'but someone else *might* have the information, there *might* be another means of saving us, the virus *might* die out of its own accord, the world *might* even plunge into the sun first – and I should have lost my job to no purpose. Translate that into political terms and governmental levels. Obviously, if we don't find a way of stopping the virus, the only sensible thing to do is plant potatoes in every spot of ground that will take them. But at what stage does one decide that the virus can't be stopped? And if we stud England's green and pleasant land with potato patches, and then someone kills the virus after all – what do you imagine the electorate is going to say when it is offered potatoes instead of bread next year?'

'I don't know what it would say. I know what it should say, though – thank God for not being reduced to cannibalism as the Chinese were.'

'Gratitude,' Roger said, 'is not the most conspicuous aspect of national life – not, at any rate, seen from the politician's eye view.'

John let his gaze travel again beyond the open door of the inn. On the green on the other side of the road, a group of village boys were playing cricket. Their voices seemed to carry to the listener on shafts of sunlight.

'We're probably both being a bit alarmist,' he said. 'It's a long cry from the news that Phase 5 is out and about to a prospect either of a potato diet or famine and cannibalism. From the time the scientists really got to work on it, it only took three months to develop 717.'

'Yes,' Roger said, 'that's something that worries me, too. Every government in the world is going to be comforting itself with the same reassuring thought. The scientists have never failed us yet. We shall never really believe they will until they do.'

'When a thing has never failed before, it's not a bad presumption that it won't fail now.'

'No,' Roger said, 'I suppose not.' He lifted his nearly empty glass. 'Look thy last on all things lovely every hour. A world without beer? Unimaginable. Drink up and let's have another.'

THREE

THE news of Phase 5 of the Chung-Li virus leaked out during the summer, and was followed by widespread rioting in those parts of the Far East that were nearest to the focus of infection. The Western world looked on with benevolent concern. Grain was shipped to the troubled areas, where armoured divisions were needed to protect it. Meanwhile, the efforts to destroy the virus continued in laboratories and field research stations all over the world.

Farmers were instructed to keep the closest possible watch for signs of the virus, with the carefully calculated prospects of heavy fines for failure to report, and good compensation for the destruction of virus-stricken crops. It had been established that Phase 5, like the original virus, travelled both by root contact and through the air. By a policy of destroying infected crops and clearing the ground for some distance around them, it was hoped to keep the spread of the virus in check until a means could be found of eradicating it entirely.

The policy was moderately successful. Phase 5, like its predecessors, reached across the world, but something like three-quarters of a normal harvest was gathered in the West. In the East, things went less well. By August, it was clear that India was faced with an overwhelming failure of crops, and a consequent famine. Burma and Japan were very little better off.

In the West, the question of relief for the stricken areas began to show a different aspect. World reserve stocks had already been drastically reduced in the attempt, in the spring, to succour China. Now, with the prospect of a poor harvest even in the least affected areas, what had been instinctive became a matter for argument.

At the beginning of September, the United States House of Representatives passed an amendment to a Presidential bill of food aid, calling for a Plimsoll line for food stocks for home use. A certain minimum tonnage of all foods was to be kept in reserve, to be used inside the United States only.

Ann could not keep her indignation at this to herself.

'Millions facing famine,' she said, 'and those fat old men refuse them food.'

They were all having tea on the Buckleys' lawn. The children had retired, with a supply of cakes, into the shrubbery, from which shrieks and giggles issued at intervals.

'As one who hopes to live to be a fat old man,' Roger said, 'I'm not sure I ought not to resent that.'

'You must admit it has a callous ring to it,' John said.

'Any act of self-defence has. The trouble as far as the Americans are concerned is that their cards are always on the table. The other grain-producing countries will just sit on their stocks without saying anything.'

Ann said: 'I can't believe that.'

'Can't you? Let me know when the Russians send their next grain ship east. I've got a couple of old hats that might as well be eaten.'

'Even so – there's Canada, Australia, New Zealand.'

'Not if they pay any attention to the British Government.'

'Why should our government tell them not to send relief?'

'Because we may want it ourselves. We are earnestly – I might say, desperately – hoping that blood is thicker than the water which separates us. If the virus isn't licked by next summer ... '

'But these people are starving now!'

'They have our deepest sympathy.'

She stared at him, for once in undisguised dislike. 'How can you!'

Roger stared back. 'We once agreed about my being a throwback – remember? If I irritate the people round me, don't forget they may irritate me occasionally. Woolly-mindedness does. I believe in self-preservation, and I'm not prepared to wait until the knife is at my throat before I start fighting. I don't see the sense in giving the children's last crust to a starving beggar.'

'Last crust ... ' Ann looked at the table, covered with the remains of a lavish tea. 'Is that what you call this?'

Roger said: 'If I were giving the orders in this country, there wouldn't have been any cake for the past three months, and precious little bread either. And I still wouldn't have had any grain to spare for the Asiatics. Good God! Don't you people ever look at the economic facts of this country?'

'If we stand by and let those millions starve without lifting a finger to help, then we deserve to have the same happen to us,' Ann said.

'Do we?' Roger asked. 'Who are we? Should Mary and Davey and Steve die of starvation because I'm callous?'

Olivia said: 'I really think it's best not to talk about it. It isn't as though there's anything we can do about it – we ourselves, anyway. We must just hope things don't turn out quite so badly.'

'According to the latest news,' John said, 'they've got something which gives very good results against Phase 5.'

'Exactly!' Ann said. 'And that being so, what justification can there possibly be for not sending help to the East? That we might have to be rationed next summer?'

'Very good results,' Roger said ironically. 'Did you know they've uncovered three further phases, beyond 5? Personally, I can see only one hope – holding out till the virus dies on its own account, of old age. They do sometimes. Whether there will be a blade of grass left to re-start things with at that stage is another thing again.'

Olivia bent down, looking at the lawn on which their chairs rested.

'It's hard to believe,' she said, 'isn't it – that it really does kill all the grass where it gets a foothold?'

Roger plucked a blade of grass, and held it between his fingers and thumb.

'I've been accused of having no imagination,' he said. 'That's not true, anyway. I can visualize the starving Indians, all right. But I can also visualize this land brown and bare, stripped and desert, and children here chewing the bark off trees.'

For a while they all sat silent; a silence of speech, but accompanied by distant bird-song and the excited happy cries of the children.

John said: 'We'd better be getting back. I've got the car to go over. I've been putting it off too long as it is.' He called out for Mary and David. 'It may never happen, Rodge, you know.'

Roger said: 'I'm as slack as the rest of you. I should be getting into training by learning unarmed combat, and the best way to slice the human body into its constituent joints for roasting. As it is, I just sit around.'

On their way home, Ann said suddenly:

'It's a beastly attitude to take up. Beastly!'

John nodded his head, warningly, towards the children.

Ann said: 'Yes, all right. But it's horrible.'

'He talks a lot,' John said. 'It doesn't mean anything, really.'

'I think it does.'

'Olivia was right, you know. There isn't anything we can do individually. Just wait and see, and hope for the best.'

'Hope for the best? Don't tell me you've started taking notice of his gloomy prophecies!'

Not answering immediately, John looked at the scattering autumn leaves and the neat suburban grass. The car travelled past a place where, for a space of ten or fifteen yards, the grass had been uprooted, leaving bare earth: another minor battlefield in the campaign against Phase 5.

'No, I don't think so, really. It couldn't happen, could it?'

As autumn settled into winter, the news from the East steadily worsened. First India, then Burma and Indo-China relapsed into famine and barbarism. Japan and the eastern states of the Soviet Union went shortly afterwards, and Pakistan erupted into a desperate wave of Western conquest which, composed though it was of starving and unarmed vagabonds, reached into Turkey before it was halted.

Those countries which were still relatively unaffected by the Chung-Li virus, stared at the scene with a barely credulous horror. The official news accentuated the size of this ocean of famine, in which any succour could be no more than a drop, but avoided the question of whether food could in fact be spared to help the victims. And those who agitated in favour of sending supplies were a minority, and a minority increasingly unpopular as the extent of the disaster penetrated more clearly, and its spread to the Western world was more clearly envisaged.

It was not until near Christmas that grain ships sailed for the East again. This followed the heartening news from the southern hemisphere that in Australia and New Zealand a vigilant system of inspection and destruction was keeping the virus under control. The summer being a particularly brilliant one, there were prospects of a harvest only a little below average.

With this news came a new wave of optimism. The disaster in the East, it was explained, had been due as much as anything to the kind of failure in thoroughness that might be expected of Asiatics. It might not be possible to keep the virus out of the fields altogether, but the Australians and New Zealanders had shown that it could be held in check there. With a similar vigilance, the West might survive indefinitely on no worse than short commons. Meanwhile, the laboratory fight against the virus was still on. Every day was one day nearer the moment of triumph over the invisible enemy. It was in this atmosphere of sober optimism that the Custances made their customary trip northwards, to spend Christmas in Blind Gill.

On their first morning, John walked out with his brother on the rounds of the farm.

They encountered the first bare patch less than a hundred yards from the farm-house. It was about ten feet across; the black frozen soil stared nakedly at the winter sky.

John went over it curiously, and David followed him.

'Have you had much of it up here?' John asked.

'Perhaps a dozen like this.'

The grass around the verges of the gash, although frost-crackled, was clearly sound enough.

'It looks as though you're holding it all right.'

David shook his head. 'Doesn't mean anything. There's a fair degree of evidence that the virus only spreads in the growing season, but nobody knows whether that means it can remain latent in the plant in the non-growing season, or not. God knows what spring will bring. A good three-quarters of my own little plague spots were end-of-season ones.'

'Then you aren't impressed by the official optimism?'

David jerked his stick towards the bare earth. 'I'm impressed by *that*.'

'They'll beat it. They're bound to.'

'There was an Order-in-Council,' David said, 'stating that all land previously cropped with grain should be turned over to potatoes.'

John nodded. 'I heard of it.'

'It's just been cancelled. On the News last night.'

'They must be confident things are going to be all right.'

David said grimly: 'They can be as confident as they like. Next spring I'm planting potatoes and beet.'

'No wheat, barley?'

'Not an acre.'

John said thoughtfully: 'If the virus is beaten by then, grain's going to fetch a high price.'

'Do you think a few other people haven't thought of that? Why do you think the Order's been rescinded?'

'It isn't easy, is it?' John asked. 'If they prohibit grain crops and the virus is beaten, this country will have to buy all its grain overseas, and at fancy prices.'

'It's a pretty gamble,' David said, ' – the life of the country against higher taxes.'

'The odds must be very good.'

David shook his head. 'They're not good enough for me. I'll stick to potatoes.'

David returned to the subject on the afternoon of Christmas Day. Mary and young David had gone out into the frosty air to work off the effects of a massive Christmas dinner. The three adults, preferring a more placid mode of digestion, lay back in armchairs, half-heartedly listening to a Haydn symphony on gramophone records.

'How did your monstrosity go, John?' David asked. 'Did you get it finished on time?'

John nodded. 'I almost retched when I contemplated it in all its hideousness. But I think the one we're on now will be able to give it a few points for really thoroughgoing ugliness.'

'Do you have to do it?'

'We must take our commissions where they lie. Even an architect has to accommodate himself to the whims of the man with the money to spend, and I'm only an engineer.'

'You're not tied, though, are you – personally tied?'

'Only to the need for money.'

'If you wanted to take a sabbatical year, you could?'

'Of course. There's just the odd problem of keeping the family out of the gutter.'

'I'd like you to come up here for a year.'

John sat up, startled. 'What?'

'You would be doing me a favour. You needn't worry about the financial side of things. There's only three things a farmer can do with his ill-gotten gains – buy fresh land, spend them on riotous living, or hoard them. I've never wanted to have land outside the valley, and I'm a poor spender.'

John said slowly: 'Is this because of the virus?'

'It may be silly,' David said, 'but I don't like the look of things. And I've seen those pictures of what happened in the East.'

John looked across at Ann. She said:

'That was the East, though, wasn't it? Even if things were to get short – this country's more disciplined. We've been used to rationing and shortages. And at present there's no sign of any real trouble. It's asking rather a lot for John to throw things in and all of us to come and sponge on you for a year – just because things might go wrong.'

'Here we are,' David said, 'sitting round the fire, at peace and with full bellies. I know it's hard to imagine a future in which we shan't be able to go on doing that. But I'm worried.'

'There's never been a disease yet,' John said, 'either of plant or animal, that hasn't run itself out, leaving the species still alive and kicking. Look at the Black Death.'

David shook his head. 'Guess-work. We don't know. What killed the great reptiles? Ice-ages? Competition? It could have been a virus. And what happened to all the plants that have left fossil remains but no descendants? It's dangerous to argue from the fact that we haven't come across such a virus in our short period of observation. A man could live a long life without seeing a comet visible to the naked eye. It doesn't mean there aren't any comets.'

John said, with an air of finality: 'It's very good of you, Dave, but I couldn't, you know. I may not care for its results, but I like my work well enough. How would you like to spend a year in Highgate, sitting on your behind?'

'I'd make a farmer out of you in a month.'

'Out of Davey, maybe.'

The clock that ticked somnolently on the wall had rested there, spring cleanings apart, for a hundred and fifty years. The notion of the virus winning, Ann thought, was even more unlikely here than it had seemed in London.

She said: 'After all, I suppose we could come up here if things were to get bad. But there's no sign of them doing so at present.'

'I've been brooding about it, I expect,' David said. 'There was something Grandfather Beverley said to me, the first time we came to the valley – that when he had been outside, and came back through the gap, he always felt that he could shut the door behind him.'

'It is a bit like that,' Ann said.

'If things do turn out badly,' David went on, 'there aren't going to be many safe refuges in England. But this can be one of them.'

'Hence the potatoes and beet,' John observed.

David said: 'And more.' He looked at them. 'Did you see that stack of timber by the road, just this side of the gap?'

'New buildings?'

David stood up and walked across to look out of the window on the wintry landscape. Still looking out, he said:

'No. Not buildings. A stockade.'

Ann and John looked at each other. Ann repeated:

'A stockade?'

David swung round. 'A fence, if you like. There's going to be a gate on this valley – a gate that can be held by a few against a mob.'

'Are you serious?' John asked him.

He watched this elder brother who had always been so much less adventurous, less imaginative, than himself. His manner now was as stolid and unexcited as ever; he hardly seemed concerned about the implications of what he had just said.

'Quite serious,' David said.

Ann protested: 'But if things turn out all right, after all ... '

'The countryside,' David said, 'is always happy to have something to laugh at. Custance's Folly. I'm taking a chance on looking a fool. I've got an uneasiness in my bones, and I'm concerned with quietening it. Being a laughing-stock doesn't count beside that.'

His quiet earnestness impressed them; they were conscious – Ann particularly – of an impulse to do as he had urged them: to join him here in the valley and fasten the gate on the jostling uncertain world outside. But the impulse could only be brief; there was all the business of life to remember. Ann said involuntarily:

'The children's schools ...'

David had followed the line of her thought; he showed neither surprise nor satisfaction. He said:

'There's the school at Lepeton. A year of that wouldn't hurt them.'

She looked helplessly at her husband. John said:

'There are all sorts of things ... ' The conviction communicated from David had already faded; the sort of thing he was imagining could not possibly happen. 'After all, if things should get worse, we shall have plenty of warning. We could come up right away, if it looked grim.'

'Don't leave it too late,' David said.

Ann gave a little shiver, and shook herself. 'In a year's time, all this will seem strange.'

'Yes,' David said, 'may be it will.'

FOUR

THE lull which seemed to have fallen on the world continued through the winter. In the Western countries, schemes for rationing foods were drawn up, and in some cases applied. Cakes disappeared in England, but bread was still available to all. The Press continued to oscillate between optimism and pessimism, but with less violent swings. The important question, most frequently canvassed, was the length of time that could be expected to ensue before, with the destruction of the virus, life might return to normal.

It was significant, John thought, that no one spoke yet of the reclamation of the lifeless lands of Asia. He mentioned this to Roger Buckley over luncheon, one day in late February. They were in Roger's club, the Treasury.

Roger said: 'No, we try not to think of them too much, don't we? It's as though we had managed to chop off the rest of the world, and left just Europe, Africa, Australasia, and the Americas. I saw some pictures of Central China last week. Even up to a few months ago, they would have been in the Press. But they haven't been published, and they're not going to be published.'

'What were they like?'

'They were in colour. Tasteful compositions in browns and greys and yellows. All that bare earth and clay. Do you know – in its way, it was more frightening than the famine pictures used to be?'

The waiter padded up and gave them their lagers in slow and patient ritual. When he had gone, John queried:

'Frightening?'

'They frightened me. I hadn't understood properly before quite what a clean sweep the virus makes of a place. Automatically, you think of it as leaving *some* grass growing. If only a few tufts here and there. But it doesn't leave anything. It's only the grasses that have gone, of course, but it's surprising to realize what a large amount of territory is covered with grasses of one kind or another.'

'Any rumours of an answer to it?'

Roger waggled his head in an indeterminate gesture. 'Let's put it this way: the rumours in official circles are as vague as the ones in the Press, but they do have a note of confidence.'

John said: 'My brother is barricading himself in. Did I tell you?'

Roger leaned forward, curiously. 'The farmer? How do you mean – barricading himself in?'

'I've told you about his place – Blind Gill – surrounded by hills with just one narrow gap leading out. He's having a fence put up to seal the gap.'

'Go on. I'm interested.'

'That's all there is to it, really. He's uneasy about what's going to happen in the next growing season – I've never known him so uneasy. At any rate, he's given up all his wheat acreage to plant root crops. He even wanted us all to come and spend a year up there.'

'Until the crisis is over? He *is* worried.'

'And yet,' John said, 'I've been thinking about it off and on since then ... Dave's always been more level-headed than I, and when you get down to it, a countryman's premonitions are not to be taken lightly in this kind of business. In London, we don't know anything except what's spooned out to us.'

Roger looked at him, and smiled. 'Something in what you say, Johnny, but you must remember that I'm on the spooning side. Tell me – if I get you the inside warning of the crack-up in plenty of time, do you think you could make room for our little trio in your brother's bolt-hole?'

John said tensely: 'Do you think it's going to come to a crack-up?'

'So far, there's not a sign of it. Those who should be in the know are radiating the same kind of optimism that you find in the papers. But I like the sound of Blind Gill, as an insurance policy. I'll keep my ear to the pipeline. As soon as there's a little warning tinkle at the other end, we both take indefinite leave, and our families, and head for the north? How does it strike you? Would your brother have us?'

'Yes, of course.' John thought about the idea. 'How much warning do you think you would get?'

'Enough. I'll keep you informed. In a case like this, you can rest assured I shall err on the side of caution. I don't relish the idea of being caught in the London area in the middle of a famine.'

A trolley was pushed past them, laden with assorted cheeses. The air was instilled with the drowsy somnolence of midday in the dining-room of a London club. The murmur of voices was an easy and untroubled one.

John waved an arm. 'It's difficult to imagine anything denting this.'

Roger surveyed the scene in turn, his eyes mild but acute.

'Quite undentable, I agree. After all, as the Press has told us sufficiently often, we're not Asiatics. It's going to be interesting, watching us being British and stiff-lipped, while the storm-clouds gather. Undentable. But what happens when we crack?'

Their waiter came with their chops. He was a garrulous little man, with less *hauteur* than most of the others there.

'No,' Roger said, 'interesting – but not interesting enough to make me want to stop and see it.'

Spring was late in coming; a period of dry, cold, cloudy weather lasted through March and into April. When, in the second week of April, it was succeeded by a warm, moist spell, it was a shock to see that the Chung-Li virus had lost none of its vigour. As the grass grew, in fields or gardens or highways, its blades were splotched with darker green – green that spread and turned into rotting brown. There was no escaping the evidence of these new inroads.

John got hold of Roger.

He asked him: 'What's the news at your end?'

'Oddly enough, very good.'

John said: 'My lawn's full of it. I started cutting-out operations but then I saw that all the grass in the district's got it.'

'Mine, too,' Roger said. 'A warm putrefying shade of brown. The penalties for failing to cut out infected grasses are being rescinded, by the way.'

'What's the good news, then? It looks grim enough to me.'

'The papers will be carrying it tomorrow. The Bureau UNESCO set up claim they've got the answer. They've bred a virus that feeds on Chung-Li – all phases.'

John said: 'It comes at what might otherwise have been a decidedly awkward moment. You don't think ... ?'

Roger smiled. 'It was the first thing I did think. But the bulletin announcing it has been signed by a gang of people, including some who wouldn't falsify the results of a minor experiment to save their aged parents from the stake. It's genuine, all right.'

'Saved by the bell,' John said slowly. 'I don't like to think what would have happened this summer otherwise.'

'I don't mind thinking about it,' Roger said. 'It was participation I was anxious to avoid.'

'I was wondering about sending the children back to school. I suppose it's all right now.'

'Better there, I should think,' Roger said. 'There are bound to be shortages, because they will hardly be able to get the new virus going on a large enough scale to do much about saving this year's harvest. London will feel the pinch more than most places, probably.'

The UNESCO report was given the fullest publicity, and the Government at the same time issued its own appraisal of the situation. The United States, Canada, Australia, and New Zealand all held grain stocks and were all prepared to impose rationing on their own populations with a view to making these stocks last over the immediate period of shortage. In Britain, a similar but more severe rationing of grain products and meat was introduced.

Once again the atmosphere lightened. The combination of news of an answer to the virus and news of the imposition of rationing produced an effect both bracing and hopeful. When a letter came from David, its tone appeared almost ludicrously out of key.

He wrote:

'There isn't a blade of grass left in the valley. I killed the last of the cows yesterday – I understand that someone in London had the sense to arrange for an extension of refrigeration space during last winter, but it won't be enough to cope with the beef that will be coming under the knife in the next few weeks. I'm salting mine. Even if things go right, it will be years before this country knows what meat is again – or milk, or cheese.

'And I wish I could believe that things are going to go right. It's not that I disbelieve this report – I know the reputation of the people who have signed it – but reports don't seem to mean very much when I can look out and see black instead of green.

'Don't forget you're welcome any time you decide to pack your things up and come. I'm not really bothered about the valley. We can live on root crops and pork – I'm keeping the pigs going because they're the only animals I know that might thrive on a diet of potatoes. We'll manage very well here. It's the land outside I'm worried about.'

John threw the letter across to Ann and went to look out of the window of the sitting-room. Ann frowned as she read it.

'He's still taking it all terribly seriously, isn't he?' she asked.

'Evidently.'

John looked out at what had been the lawn and was now a patch of brown earth speckled with occasional weeds. Already it had become familiar.

'You don't think,' Ann said, 'living up there with only the Hillens and the farm men ... it's a pity he never married.'

'He's going off his rocker, you mean? He's not the only pessimist about the virus.'

'This bit at the end,' Ann said. She quoted:

'In a way, I think I feel it would be more *right* for the virus to win, anyway. For years now, we've treated the land as though it were a piggy-bank, to be raided. And the land, after all, is life itself.'

John said: 'We're cushioned – we never did see a great deal of grass, so not seeing any doesn't make much difference. It's bound to have a more striking effect in the country.'

'But it's almost as though he *wants* the virus to win.'

'The countryman always has disliked and mistrusted the townsman. He sees him as a gaping mouth on top of a lazy body. I suppose most farmers would be happy enough to see the urban dweller take a small tumble. Only this tumble, if it were taken, would be anything but small. I don't think David wants Chung-Li to beat us, though. He's just got it on his mind.'

Ann was silent for a while. John looked round at her. She was staring at the blank screen of the television set, with David's letter tightly held in one hand.

'It may be he's getting a bit of a worriter in his old age. Bachelor farmers often do.'

Ann said: 'This idea – of Roger warning us if things go wrong so that we can all travel north – is it still on?'

John said curiously: 'Yes, of course. Though it hardly seems pressing now.'

'Can we rely on him?'

'Don't you think so? Even if he were willing to take chances with our lives, do you think he would with his own – and with Olivia's, and Steve's?'

'I suppose not. It's just ...'

'If there were going to be trouble, we shouldn't need Roger's warning, anyway. We should see it coming, a mile off.'

Ann said: 'I was thinking about the children.'

'They'll be all right. Davey even likes the tinned hamburger the Americans are sending us.'

Ann smiled. 'Yes, we've always got the tinned hamburger to fall back on, I suppose.'

They went down to the sea as usual with the Buckleys when the children came back for the summer half-term holiday. It was a strange journey through a land showing only the desolate bareness of virus-choked ground, interspersed with fields where the abandoned grain crops had been replaced by roots. But the roads themselves were as thronged with traffic, and it was as difficult as ever to find a not too crowded patch of coast.

The weather was warm, but the air was dark with clouds that continually threatened rain. They did not go far from the caravan.

Their halting-place was on a spur of high ground, looking down to the shingle, and giving a wide view of the Channel. Davey and Steve showed a great interest in the traffic on the sea; there was a fleet of small vessels a couple of miles off shore.

'Fishing smacks,' Roger explained. 'To make up for the meat we haven't got, because there isn't any grass for the cows.'

'And rationed from Monday,' Olivia said. 'Fancy – fish rationed!'

'It was about time,' Ann commented. 'The prices were getting ridiculous.'

'The smooth mechanism of the British national economy continues to mesh with silent efficiency,' Roger said. 'They told us that we were different from the Asiatics, and by God they were right! The belt tightens notch by notch, and no one complains.'

'There wouldn't be much point in complaining, would there?' Ann asked.

John said: 'It's rather different now that the ultimate prospects are fairly good. I don't know how calm and collected we should be if they weren't.'

Mary, who had been drying herself in the caravan after a bathe, looked out of the window at them.

'The fishcakes at school always used to be a tin of anchovies to twenty pounds of potatoes – now it's more like a tin to two hundred pounds. What are the ultimate prospects of that, Daddy?'

'Potato-cakes,' John said, 'and the empty tin circulating along the tables for you all to have a sniff. Very nourishing too.'

Davey said: 'Well, I don't see why they've rationed sweets. You don't get sweets out of grass, do you?'

'Too many people had started to fill up on them,' John told him. 'You included. Now you're confined to your own ration, and what Mary doesn't get of your mother's and mine. Contemplate your good fortune. You might be an orphan.'

'Well, how long's the rationing going to go on?'

'A few years yet, so you'd better get used to it.'

'It's a swindle,' Davey said, ' – rationing, without even the excitement of there being a war on.'

The children went back to school, and for the rest life continued as usual. At one time, soon after they had made their pact, John had made a point of telephoning Roger whenever two or three days went by without their meeting, but now he did not bother.

Food rationing tightened gradually, but there was enough food to stay the actual pangs of hunger. There was news that in some other countries similarly situated, food riots had taken place, notably in the countries bordering the Mediterranean. London reacted smugly to this, contrasting that indiscipline with its own patient and orderly queues for goods in short supply.

'Yet again,' a correspondent wrote to the *Daily Telegraph*, 'it falls to the British peoples to set an example to the world in the staunch and steadfast bearing of their misfortunes. Things may grow darker yet, but that patience and fortitude is something we know will not fail.'

FIVE

JOHN had gone down to the site of their new building, which was rising on the edge of the City. Trouble had developed on the tower-crane, and everything was held up as a result. His presence was not strictly required, but he had been responsible for the selection of a crane, which was of a type they had not used previously, and he wanted to be on the spot.

He was actually in the cabin of the crane, looking down into the building's foundations, when he saw Roger waving to him from the ground. He waved back, and Roger's gestures changed to a beckoning that even from that height could be recognized as imperative.

He turned to the mechanic who was working beside him. 'How's she coming now?'

'Bit better. Clear it this morning, I reckon.'

'I'll be back later on.'

Roger was waiting for him at the bottom of the ladder.

John said: 'Dropped in to see what kind of a mess we were in?'

Roger did not smile. He glanced round the busy levels of the site.

'Anywhere we can talk privately?'

John shrugged. 'I could clear the manager out of his cubby-hole. But there's a little pub just across the road, which would be better.'

'Anywhere you like. But right away. O.K.?'

Roger's face was as mild and relaxed as ever, but his voice was sharp and urgent. They went across the road together. 'The Grapes' had a small private bar which was not much used and now, at eleven-thirty, was empty.

John got double whiskies for them both and brought them to the table, in the corner farthest from the bar, where Roger was sitting. He asked:

'Bad news?'

'We've got to move,' Roger said. He had a drink of whisky. 'The balloon's up.'

'How?'

'The bastards!' Roger said. 'The bloody murdering bastards. We aren't like the Asiatics. We're true-blue Englishmen and we play cricket.'

His anger, bitter and savage, with nothing feigned in it, brought home to John the awareness of crisis. He said sharply:

'What is it? What's happening?'

Roger finished his drink. The barmaid passed through their section of the bar and he called for two more doubles. When he had got them, he said:

'First things first – game, set, and match to Chung-Li. We've lost.'

'What about the counter-virus?'

'Funny things, viruses,' Roger said. 'They stand in time's eye like principalities and powers, only on a shorter scale. All-conquering for a century, or for three or four months, and then – washed out. You don't often get a Rome, holding its power for half a millennium.'

'Well?'

'The Chung-Li virus is a Rome. If the counter-virus had been even a France or a Spain it would have been all right. But it was only a Sweden. It still exists, but in the mild and modified form that viruses usually relapse into. It won't touch Chung-Li.'

'When did this happen?'

'God knows. Some time ago. They managed to keep it quiet while they were trying to re-breed the virulent strain.'

'They've not abandoned the attempt, surely?'

'I don't know. I suppose not. It doesn't matter.'

'Surely it matters.'

'For the last month,' Roger said, 'this country has been living on current supplies of food, with less than half a week's stocks behind us. In fact, we've been relying absolutely on the food ships from America and the Commonwealth. I knew this before, but I didn't think it important. The food has been pledged to us.'

The barmaid returned and began to polish the bar counter; she was whistling a popular song. Roger dropped his voice.

'My mistake was pardonable, I think. In normal circumstances the pledges would have been honoured. Too much of the world had vanished into barbarism already; people were willing to make some sacrifices to save the rest.

'But charity still begins at home. That's why I said it doesn't matter whether they do succeed in getting the counter-virus back in shape. The fact is that the people who've got the food don't believe they will. And as a result, they want to make sure they aren't giving away stuff they will need themselves next winter. The last foodship from the other side of the Atlantic docked at Liverpool yesterday. There may be some still on the seas from Australasia, and they may or may not be recalled home before they reach us.'

John said: 'I see.' He looked at Roger. 'Is that what you meant about murdering bastards? But they do have to look after their own people. It's hard on us ...'

'No, that wasn't what I meant. I told you I had a pipe-line up to the top. It was Haggerty, the P.M.'s secretary. I did him a good turn a few years ago. He's done me a damn sight better turn in giving me the lowdown on what's happening.

'Everything's been at top-Governmental level. Our people knew what was going to happen a week ago. They've been trying to get the food-suppliers to change their minds – and hoping for a miracle, I suppose. But all they did get was secrecy – an undertaking that they would not be embarrassed in any steps they thought necessary for internal control by the news being spread round the world. That suited everybody's book – the people across the ocean will have some measures of their own to take before the news breaks – not comparable with ours, of course, but best-prepared undisturbed.'

'And our measures?' John asked. 'What are they?'

'The Government fell yesterday. Welling has taken over, but Lucas is still in the Cabinet. It's very much a palace revolution. Lucas doesn't want the blood on his hands – that's all.'

'Blood?'

'These islands hold about fifty-four million people. About forty-five million of them live in England. If a third of that number could be supported on a diet of roots, we should be doing well. The only difficulty is – how do you select the survivors?'

John said grimly: 'I should have thought it was obvious – they select themselves.'

'It's a wasteful method, and destructive of good order and discipline. We've taken our discipline fairly lightly in this country, but its roots run deep. It's always likely to rise in a crisis.'

'Welling – ' John said, 'I've never cared for the sound of him.'

'The time throws up the man. I don't like the swine myself, but something like him was inevitable. Lucas could never make up his mind about anything.' Roger looked straight ahead. 'The Army is moving into position today on the outskirts of London and all other major population centres. The roads will be closed from dawn tomorrow.'

John said: 'If that's the best he can think of ... no army in the world would stop a city from bursting out under pressure of hunger. What does he think he's going to gain?'

'Time. Enough of that precious commodity to complete the preparations for his second line of action.'

'And that is?'

'Atom bombs for the small cities, hydrogen bombs for places like Liverpool, Birmingham, Glasgow, Leeds – and two or three of them for London. It doesn't matter about wasting them – they won't be needed in the foreseeable future.'

For a moment, John was silent. Then he said slowly:

'I can't believe that. No one could do that.'

'Lucas couldn't. Lucas always was the common man's Prime Minister – suburban constraints and suburban prejudices and emotions. But Lucas will stand by as a member of Welling's Cabinet, ostentatiously washing his hands while the plans go forward. What else do you expect of the common man?'

'They will never get people to man the planes.'

'We're in a new era,' Roger said. 'Or a very old one. Wide loyalties are civilized luxuries. Loyalties are going to be narrow from now on, and the narrower the fiercer. If it were the only way of saving Olivia and Steve, I'd man one of those planes myself.'

Revolted, John said: 'No!'

'When I spoke about murdering bastards,' Roger said, 'I spoke with admiration as well as disgust. From now on, I propose to be one where necessary, and I very much hope you are prepared to do the same.'

'But to drop hydrogen bombs on cities – of one's own people ...'

'Yes, that's what Welling wants time for. I should think it will take at least twenty-four hours – perhaps as long as forty-eight. Don't be a fool, Johnny! It's not so long ago that one's own people were the people in the same village. As a matter of fact, he can put a good cloak of generosity over the act.'

'Generosity? Hydrogen bombs?'

'They're going to die. In England, at least thirty million people are going to die before the rest can scrape a living. Which way's best – of starvation or being killed for your flesh – or by a hydrogen bomb? It's quick, after all. And you can keep the numbers down to thirty million that way and preserve the fields to grow the crops to support the rest. That's the theory of it.'

From another part of the public-house, light music came to them as the barmaid switched on a portable wireless. The ordinary world continued, untouched, untroubled.

'It can't work,' John said.

'I'm inclined to agree,' said Roger. 'I think the news will leak, and I think the cities will burst their seams before Welling has got his bomber fleet properly lined up. But I'm not under any illusion that things will be any better that way. At my guess, it means fifty million dying instead of thirty, and a far more barbarous and primitive existence for those that do survive. Who is going to have the power to protect the potato fields against the roaming mob? Who is going to save seed potatoes for next year? Welling's a swine, but a clear-sighted swine. After his fashion, he's trying to save the country.'

'You think the news will get out?'

In his mind he visualized a panic-stricken London, with himself and Ann caught in it – unable to get to the children.

Roger grinned. 'Worrying, isn't it? It's a funny thing, but I have an idea we shall worry less about London's teeming millions once we're away from them. And the sooner we get away, the better.'

John said: 'The children ...'

'Mary at Beckenham, and Davey at that place in Hertfordshire. I've thought about that. We can get Davey on the way north. Your job is to go and pick Mary up. Right away. I'll go and get word to Ann. She can pack essentials. Olivia and Steve and I will be at your place, with our car loaded. When you get there with Mary, we'll load your car and get moving. If possible, we should be clear of London well before nightfall.'

'I suppose we must,' John said.

Roger followed his gaze round the interior of the bar – flowers in a polished copper urn, a calendar blowing in a small breeze, floors still damp from scrubbing.

'Say goodbye to it,' he said. 'That's yesterday's world. From now on, we're peasants, and lucky at that.'

Beckenham, Roger had told him, was included in the area to be sealed off. He was shown into the study of Miss Errington, the headmistress, and waited there for her. The room was neat, but still feminine. It was a combination, he remembered, that had impressed Ann, as Miss Errington herself had done. She was a very tall woman, with a gentle humorousness.

She bowed her head coming through the door, and said:

'Good afternoon, Mr Custance.' It was, John noted, just half an hour after noon. 'I'm sorry to have kept you waiting.'

'I hope I haven't brought you away from your luncheon?'

She smiled. 'It is no hardship these days, Mr Custance. You've come about Mary?'

'Yes. I should like to take her back with me.'

Miss Errington said: 'Do have a seat.' She looked at him, calmly considerate. 'You want to take her away? Why?'

This was the moment that made him feel the bitter weight of his secret knowledge. He must give no warning of what was to happen; Roger had insisted on that, and he agreed. It was as essential to their plans as to Welling's larger scheme of destruction that no news should get out.

And that necessity required that he should leave this tall, gentle woman, along with her charges, to die.

He said lamely: 'It's a family matter. A relative, passing through London. You understand ...'

'You see, Mr Custance, we try to keep breaks of this kind to a minimum. You will appreciate that it's very unsettling. It's rather different at week-ends.'

'Yes. I do see that. It's her – uncle, and he's going abroad by air this evening.'

'Really? For long?'

More glibly, he continued: 'He may be gone for some years. He was very anxious to see Mary before he went.'

'You could have brought him here, of course.' Miss Errington hesitated. 'When would you be bringing her back?'

'I could bring her back this evening.'

'Well, in that case . . . I'll go and ask someone to get her.' She walked over to the door, and opened it. She called into the corridor: 'Helena? Would you ask Mary Custance to come along here, please? Her father has come to see her.' To John, she said: 'If it's only for the afternoon, she won't want her things, will she?'

'No,' he said, 'it doesn't matter about them.'

Miss Errington sat down again. 'I should tell you I'm very pleased with your daughter, Mr Custance. At her age, girls divide out – one sees something of what they are going to turn into. Mary has been coming along very well lately. I believe she might have a very fine academic future, if she wished.'

Academic future, John thought – to hold a tiny oasis against a desert world.

He said: 'That's very gratifying.'

Miss Errington smiled. 'Although, probably, the point is itself academic. One doubts if the young men of her acquaintance will permit her to settle into so barren a life.'

'I see nothing barren in it, Miss Errington. Your own must be very full.'

She laughed. 'It has turned out better than I thought it would! I'm beginning to look forward to my retirement.'

Mary came in, curtseyed briefly to Miss Errington, and ran over to John.

'Daddy! What's happened?'

Miss Errington said: 'Your father wishes to take you away for a few hours. Your uncle is passing through London, on his way abroad, and would like to see you.'

'Uncle David? Abroad?'

John said quickly: 'It's quite unexpected. I'll explain everything to you on the way. Are you ready to come as you are?'

'Yes, of course.'

'Then I shan't keep you,' Miss Errington said. 'Can you have her back for eight o'clock, Mr Custance?'

'I shall try my best.'

She held her long delicate hand out. 'Good-bye.'

John hesitated; his mind rebelled against taking her hand and leaving her with no inkling of what lay ahead. And yet he dared not tell her; nor, he thought, would she believe him if he did.

He said: 'If I fail to bring Mary back by eight, it will be because I have learned that the whole of London is to be swallowed up in an earthquake. So if we don't come back, I advise you to round up the girls and take them out into the country. At whatever inconvenience.'

Miss Errington looked at him with mild astonishment that he should descend into such absurd and tasteless clowning. Mary also was watching him in surprise.

The headmistress said: 'Well, yes, but of course you will be back by eight.'

He said, miserably: 'Yes, of course.'

As the car pulled out of the school grounds, Mary said:

'It isn't Uncle David, is it?'

'No.'

'What is it, then, Daddy?'

'I can't tell you yet. But we're leaving London.'

'Today? Then I shan't go back to school tonight?' He made no answer. 'Is it something dreadful?'

'Dreadful enough. We're going to live in the valley. Will you like that?'

She smiled. 'I wouldn't call it dreadful.'

'The dreadful part,' he said slowly, 'will be for other people.'

They reached home soon after two. As they walked up the garden path, Ann opened the door for them. She looked tense and unhappy. John put an arm around her.

'Stage one completed without mishap. Everything's going well, darling. Nothing to worry about. Roger and the others not here?'

'It's his car. Cylinder block cracked, or something. He's round at the garage, hurrying them up. They're all coming over as soon as possible.'

'Has he any idea how long?' John asked sharply.

'Shouldn't be more than an hour.'

Mary asked: 'Are the Buckleys coming with us? What's happening?'

Ann said: 'Run up to your room, darling. I've packed your things for you, but I've left just a little space for anything which I've left out which you think is specially important. But you will have to be very discriminating. It's only a very little space.'

'How long are we going for?'

Ann said: 'A long time, perhaps. In fact, you might as well act as though we were never coming back.'

Mary looked at them for a moment. Then she said gravely: 'What about Davey's things? Shall I look through those as well?'

'Yes, darling,' Ann said. 'See if there's anything important I've missed.'

When Mary had gone upstairs, Ann clung to her husband. 'John, it can't be true!'

'Roger told you the whole story?'

'Yes. But they couldn't do it. They couldn't possibly.'

'Couldn't they? I've just told Miss Errington I shall be bringing Mary back this evening. Knowing what I know, is there very much difference?'

Ann was silent. Then she said:

'Before all this is over . . . are we going to hate ourselves? Or are we just going to get used to things, so that we don't realize what we're turning into?'

John said: 'I don't know. I don't know anything, except that we've got to save ourselves and save the children.'

'Save them for what?'

'We can work that out later. Things seem brutal now – leaving without saying a word to all the others who don't know what's going to happen – but we can't help it. When we get to the valley, it will be different. We shall have a chance of living decently again.'

'Decently?'

'Things will be hard, but it may not be a bad life. It will be up to us what we make of it. At least, we shall be our own masters. It will no longer be a matter of living on the sufferance of a State that cheats and bullies and swindles its citizens and, at last, when they become a burden, murders them.'

'No, I suppose not.'

'Bastards!' Roger said. 'I paid them double for a rush job, and then had to hang around for three-quarters of an hour while they looked for their tools.'

It was four o'clock. Ann said:

'Have we time for a cup of tea? I was just going to put the kettle on.'

'Theoretically,' Roger said, 'we've got all the time in the world. All the same, I think we'll skip the tea. There's an atmosphere about – uneasiness. There must have been some other leaks, and I wonder just how many. Anyway, I shall feel a lot happier when we're clear of London.'

Ann nodded. 'All right.' She walked through to the kitchen. John called after her:

'Anything I can get for you?'

Ann looked back. 'I left the kettle full of water. I was just going to put it away.'

'That's our hope,' Roger said. 'The feminine stabilizer. She's leaving her home for ever, but she puts the kettle away. A man would be more likely to kick it round the floor, and then set fire to the house.'

They pulled away from the Custances' house with John's car leading, and drove to the north. They were to follow the Great North Road to a point beyond Welwyn and then branch west in the direction of Davey's school.

As they were passing through East Finchley, they heard the sound of Roger's horn, and a moment later he accelerated past them and drew up just ahead. As they went past, Olivia, leaning out of the window, called:

'Radio!'

John switched on.

'... emphasized too strongly that there is no basis to any of the rumours that have been circulating. The entire situation is under control, and the country has ample stocks of food.'

The others walked back and stood by the car. Roger said:

'Someone's worried.'

'Virus-free grain is being planted,' the voice continued, 'in several parts of England, Wales, and Scotland, and there is every expectation of a late-autumn crop.'

'Planting in July!' John exclaimed.

'Stroke of genius,' Roger said. 'When there's a rumour of bad news, say that Fairy Godmother is on her way down the chimney. Plausibility doesn't matter at a time like that.'

The announcer's voiced changed slightly:

'It is the Government's view that danger could only arise from panic in the population at large. As a measure towards preventing this, various temporary regulations have been promulgated, and come into force immediately.

'The first of these deals with restrictions on movements. Travel between cities is temporarily forbidden. It is hoped that a system of priorities for essential movements will be ready by tomorrow, but the preliminary ban is absolute ...'

Roger said: 'They've jumped the gun! Come on – let's try and crash through. They may not be ready for us yet.'

The two cars drove north again, across the North Circular Road, and through North Finchley and Barnet. The steady reassuring voice on the radio continued to drone out regulations, and then was followed by the music of a cinema organ. The streets showed their usual traffic, with people shopping or simply walking about. There was no evidence of panic here in the outer suburbs. Trouble, if there were any, would have started in Central London.

They met the road block just beyond Wrotham Park. Barriers had been set up in the road; there were khaki-clad figures on the other side. The two cars halted. John and Roger went over to the road block. Already there were half a dozen motorists there, arguing with the officer in charge. Others, having abandoned the argument, were preparing to turn their cars and drive back.

'Ten bloody minutes!' Roger said. 'We can't have missed it by more; there would have been a much bigger pile-up.'

The officer was a pleasant, rather wide-eyed young fellow, clearly enjoying what he saw as an unusual kind of exercise.

'I'm very sorry,' he was saying, 'but we're simply carrying out orders. No travel out of London is permitted.'

The man who was at the front of the objectors, about fifty, heavily built and darkly Jewish in appearance, said:

'But my business is in Sheffield! I only drove down to London yesterday.'

'You'll have to listen to the news on the wireless,' the officer said. 'They're going to have some kind of arrangements for people like you.'

Roger said quietly: 'This is no go, Johnny. We couldn't even bribe him with a mob like this around.'

The officer went on: 'Don't treat this as official, but I've been told the whole thing's only a manoeuvre. They're trying out panic precautions, just to be on the safe side. It will probably be called off in the morning.'

The heavily built man said: 'If it's only a manoeuvre, you can let a few get through. It doesn't matter, does it?'

The young officer grinned. 'Sorry. It's as easy to land a general court-martial for dereliction of duty on manoeuvres as it is when there's a war on! I advise you to go back to town and try to-morrow.'

Roger jerked his head, and he and John began to walk back to the cars. Roger said:

'Very cleverly carried out. Unofficially, only a manoeuvre. That gets over the scruples of the troops. I wonder if they are going to be left to burn with the rest? I suppose so.'

'Worth trying to tell them what's really happening?'

'Wouldn't get anywhere. And they might very well run us in for spreading false rumours. That's one of the new regulations – did you hear it?'

They reached the cars. John said:

'Then what do we do? Ditch the cars, and try it on foot, through the fields?'

Ann said: 'What's happening? They won't let us through?'

'They'll have the fields patrolled,' Roger said. 'Probably with tanks. We wouldn't have a chance on foot.'

In an edged voice, Ann said: 'Then what can we do?'

Roger looked at her, laughing. 'Easy, Annie! Everything's under control.'

John was grateful for the strength and confidence in the laugh. They lightened his own spirits.

Roger said: 'The first thing to do is get away from here, before we land ourselves in a traffic jam.' Cars were beginning to pile up behind them in the road. 'Back towards Chipping Barnet, and there's a sharp fork to the right. We'll go first. See you there.'

It was a quiet road: *urbs in rure*. The two cars pulled up in a secluded part of it. There were modern detached houses on the other side, but here the road fringed a small plantation.

The Buckleys left their car, and Olivia and Steve got in the back with Ann.

Roger said: 'Point one – this road bypasses A.1 and will take us to Hatfield. But I don't think it's worth trying it just yet. There's bound to be a road-block on it, and we would be no more likely to get through it this evening than we should have been on A.1.'

A Vanguard swept past them along the road, closely followed by an Austin which John recognized as having been at the road-block. Roger nodded after them.

'Quite a few will try it, but they won't get anywhere.'

Steve said: 'Couldn't we crash one of the barriers, Dad? I've seen them on the pictures.'

'This isn't the pictures,' Roger said. 'Quite a few people will be trying to get through the blocks this evening. It will be quieter at night, and better in other ways, too. We'll keep your car here. I'm taking ours back into Town – and there's something I think I ought to pick up.'

Ann said; 'You're not going back in there!'

'It's necessary. I hope I shan't be more than a couple of hours at the outside.'

John understood Roger too well to think that when he spoke

of picking something up he could be referring to an oversight in his original plans. This was a new factor.

He said: 'Not likely to be any trouble in a spot like this is there?' Roger shook his head. 'In that case, I'll come back with you. Two will be safer than one if you're going south.'

Roger thought about this for a moment. He said:

'Yes. O.K.'

'But you don't know what it's going to be like in London!' Ann said. 'There may be rioting. Surely there can't be anything important enough to make you take risks like that?'

'From now on,' Roger said, 'if we're going to survive we shall have to take risks. If you want to know, I'm going back for fire-arms. Things are breaking up faster than I thought they would. But there's no danger back there this evening.'

Ann said: 'I want you to stay, John.'

'Now, Ann . . . ' John began.

Roger broke in. 'If we want to kill ourselves, wasting time in wrangling is as good a way as any. This party's got to have a leader, and his word has got to be acted on as soon as it's spoken. Toss you for it, Johnny.'

'No. It's yours.'

Roger took a half-crown from his pocket. He spun it up.

'Call!'

They watched the twinkling nickel-silver. 'Heads,' John said. The coin hit the metalled road and rolled into the gutter. Roger bent down to look at it.

'All yours,' he said. 'Well?'

John kissed Ann, and then got out of the car. 'We'll be back as soon as possible,' he said.

Ann commented bitterly: 'Are we chattels again already?'

Roger laughed. 'The world's great age,' he said, 'begins anew, the golden years return.'

'We can just make it,' Roger said. 'He doesn't put up the shutters until six. Only a little business – one man and a boy – but he's got some useful stock.'

They were driving now through the chaos of rush-hour in Central London. On that chaos, the usual rough-and-ready pattern was imposed by traffic lights and white-armed policemen. There was no sign of anything out of the ordinary. As the lights turned green in front of their car, the familiar breaker of jay-walkers swelled across the road.

'Sheep,' John said bitterly, 'for the slaughter.'

Roger glanced at him. 'Let's hope they stay that way. See it clearly and see it whole. Quite a few millions have got to die. Our concern is to avoid joining them.'

Just past the lights, he pulled off the main street into a narrow side-street. It was five minutes to six.

'Will he serve us?' John asked.

Roger pulled in to the kerb, opposite a little shop displaying sporting guns. He put the car in neutral, but left the engine running.

'He will,' he said, 'one way or another.'

There was no one in the shop except the proprietor, a small hunched man, with a deferential salesman's face and incongrously watchful eyes. He looked about sixty.

Roger said: 'Evening, Mr Pirrie. Just caught you?'

Mr Pirrie's hands rested on the counter. 'Well – Mr Buckley, isn't it? Yes, I was just closing. Anything I can get you?'

Roger said: 'Well, let me see. Couple of revolvers, couple of good rifles with telescopic sights; and the ammo of course. And do you stock automatics?'

Pirrie smiled gently. 'Licence?'

Roger had advanced until he was standing on the other side of the counter from the old man. 'Do you think it's worth bothering about that?' he asked. 'You know I'm not a gunman. I want the stuff in a hurry, and I'll give you more than a fair price for it.'

Pirrie's head shook slightly; his eyes did not leave Roger's face. 'I don't do that kind of business.'

'Well, what about that little .22 over there?'

Roger pointed. Pirrie's eyes looked in the same direction, and as they did so, Roger leapt for his throat. John thought at first that the little man had caved in under the attack, but a moment later he saw him clear of Roger and standing back. His right hand held a revolver.

He said: 'Stand still, Mr Buckley. And your friend. The trouble with raiding a gunsmiths is that you are likely to encounter a man who has some small skill in handling weapons. Please don't interrupt me while I telephone.'

He had backed away until his free hand was near the telephone.

Roger said sharply: 'Wait a minute. I've got something to offer you.'

'I *don't* think so.'

'Your life?'

Pirrie's hand held the telephone handpiece, but had not yet lifted it. He smiled. 'Surely not.'

'Why do you think I tried to knock you out? You can't imagine I would do it if I weren't desperate.'

'I'm inclined to agree with you on that,' Pirrie said politely. 'I should not have let anyone else come so close to overpowering me, but one does not expect desperation in a senior Civil Servant. Not so violent a desperation, at least.'

Roger said: 'We have left our families in a car just off the Great North Road. There's room for another if you care to join us.'

'I understand,' Pirrie said, 'that travel out of London is temporarily forbidden.'

Roger nodded. 'That's one reason we wanted the arms. We're getting out tonight.'

'You didn't get the arms.'

'Your credit, not my discredit,' Roger said, 'and damn well you know it.'

Pirrie removed his hand from the telephone. 'Perhaps you would care to give me a brief explanation of your urgent need for arms and for getting out of London.'

He listened, without interrupting, while Roger talked. At the end, he said softly:

'A farm you say, in a valley? A valley that can be defended?'

'By half a dozen,' John put in, 'against an army.'

Pirrie lowered the revolver he held. 'I had a telephone call this afternoon,' he said, 'from the local Superintendent of Police. He asked me if I wanted a guard here. He seemed very concerned for my safety, and the only explanation he offered was that there were some silly rumours about, which might lead to trouble.'

'He didn't insist on a guard?' Roger asked.

'No, I suppose there would have been the disadvantage that a police guard becomes conspicuous.' He nodded politely to Roger. 'You will understand how I chanced to be so well prepared for you.'

'And now?' John pressed him. 'Do you believe us?'

Pirrie sighed. 'I believe that you believe it. Apart from that, I have been wondering myself if there were any reasonable way of getting out of London. Even without fully crediting your tale, I do not care to be compulsorily held here. And your tale does not strain my credulity as much, perhaps, as it ought. Living with guns, as I have done, one loses the habit of looking for gentleness in men.'

Roger said: 'Right. Which guns do we take?'

Pirrie turned slightly, and this time picked up the telephone. Automatically, Roger moved towards him. Pirrie looked at the gun in his hand, and tossed it to Roger.

'I am telephoning to my wife,' he said. 'We live in St John's Wood. I imagine that if you can get two cars out, you can get three? The extra vehicle may come in useful.'

He was dialling the number. Roger said warningly:

'Careful what you say over that.'

Pirrie said into the mouthpiece: 'Hello, my dear. I'm just preparing to leave. I thought it might be nice to pay a visit to the Rosenblums this evening – yes, the Rosenblums. Get things ready would you? I shall be right along.'

He replaced the receiver. 'The Rosenblums,' he explained, 'live in Leeds. Millicent is very quick to perceive things.'

Roger looked at him with respect. 'My God, she must be! I can see that both you and Millicent are going to be very useful members of the group. By the way, we had previously decided that this kind of party needs a leader.'

Pirrie nodded. 'You?'

'No. John Custance here.'

Pirrie surveyed John briefly. 'Very well. Now, the weapons. I will set them out, and you can start carrying them to your car.'

They were taking out the last of the ammunition when a police constable strolled towards them. He looked with some interest at the little boxes.

'Evening, Mr Pirrie,' he said. 'Transferring stock?'

'This is for your people,' Pirrie said. 'They asked for it. Keep an eye on the shop, will you? We'll be back for some more later on.'

'Do what I can, sir,' the policeman said doubtfully, 'but I've got a beat to cover, you know.'

Pirrie finished padlocking the front door. 'My little joke,' he said, 'but your people start the rumours.'

As they pulled away, John said: 'Lucky he didn't ask what your two helpers were up to.'

'The genus Constable,' Pirrie said, 'is very inquisitive once its curiosity is aroused. Providing you can avoid that, you have no cause to worry. Just off St John's Wood High Street. I'll direct you particularly from there.'

On Pirrie's direction, they drew up behind an ancient Ford. Pirrie called: 'Millicent!' in a clear, loud voice, and a woman got out of the car and came back to them. She was a good twenty years younger than Pirrie, about his height, with features dark and attractive, if somewhat sharp.

'Have you packed?' Pirrie asked her. 'We aren't coming back.'

She accepted this casually. She said, in a slightly Cockney voice: 'Everything we'll need, I think. What's it all about? I've asked Hilda to look after the cat.'

'Poor pussy,' said Pirrie. 'But I fear we must abandon her. I'll explain things on the way.' He turned to the other two. 'I will join Millicent from this point.'

Roger was staring at the antique car in front of them. 'I don't want to seem rude,' he said, 'but mightn't it be better if you piled your stuff in with ours? We could manage it quite easily.'

Pirrie smiled as he got out of the car. 'A left fork just short of Wrotham Park?' he queried. 'We'll find you there, shall we?'

Roger shrugged. Pirrie escorted his wife to the car ahead. Roger started up his own car and cruised slowly past them. He and John were startled, a moment later, when the Ford ripped past with an altogether improbable degree of acceleration, checked at the intersection, and then slid away on to the main road. Roger started after it, but by the time he had got into the stream of traffic it was lost to sight.

They did not see it again until they reached the Great North Road. Pirrie's Ford was waiting for them, and thereafter followed demurely.

They had their suppers separately in their individual cars. Once they were out of London, they would eat communally, but a picnic here might attract attention. They had parked at discreet distances also.

Roger had explained his plan to John, and he had approved it. By eleven o'clock the road they were in was deserted; London's outer suburbs were at rest. But they did not move until midnight. It was a moonless night, but there was light from the widely spaced lamp standards. The children slept in the rear seats of the cars. Ann sat beside John in the front.

She shivered. 'Surely there's another way of getting out?'

He stared ahead into the dim shadowy road. 'I can't think of one.'

She looked at him. 'You aren't the same person, are you? The idea of quite calmly planning murder ... it's more grotesque than horrible.'

'Ann,' he said. 'Davey is thirty miles away, but he might as well be thirty million if we let ourselves be persuaded into remaining in this trap.' He nodded his head towards the rear seat, where Mary lay bundled up. 'And it isn't only ourselves.'

'But the odds are so terribly against you.'

He laughed. 'Does that affect the morality of it? As a matter of fact, without Pirrie the odds would have been steep. I think they're quite reasonable now. A Bisley shot was just what we needed.'

'Must you shoot to kill?'

He began to say: 'It's a matter of safety ... ' He felt the car creak over; Roger had come up quietly and was leaning on the open window.

'O.K.?' Roger asked. 'We've got Olivia and Steve in with Millicent.'

John got out of the car. He said to Ann:

'Remember – you and Millicent bring these cars up as soon as you hear the horn. You can feel your way forward a little if you like, but it will carry well enough at this time of night.'

Ann stared up to him. 'Good luck.'

'Nothing in it,' he said.

They went back to Roger's car, where Pirrie was already waiting. Then Roger drove slowly forward, past John's parked car, along the deserted road. It had already been reconnoitred earlier in the evening, and they knew where the last bend before the road-block was. They stopped there, and John and Pirrie slipped out and disappeared into the night. Five minutes later, Roger restarted the engine and accelerated noisily towards the road-block.

Reconnaissance had shown the block to be held by a corporal and two soldiers. Two of these could be presumed to be sleeping; the third stood by the wooden barrier, his automatic slung from his shoulder.

The car slammed to a halt. The guard hefted his automatic into a readier position.

Roger leaned out of the window. He shouted:

'What the hell's that bloody contraption doing in the middle of the road? Get it shifted, man!'

He sounded drunk, and verging on awkwardness. The guard called down:

'Sorry, sir. Road closed. All roads out of London closed.'

'Well, get the flaming things open again! Get this one open, anyway. I want to get home.'

From his position in the left-hand ditch, John watched. Strangely, he felt no particular tension; he floated free, attached to the scene only by admiration of Roger's noisy expostulation.

Another figure appeared beside the original soldier and, after a moment, a third. The car's headlights diffused upwards off the metalled road; the three figures were outlined, mistily but with reasonable definition, on the other side of the wooden barrier. A second voice, presumably the corporal's said:

'We're carrying out orders. We don't want any trouble. You clear off back, mate. All right?'

'Is it hell all right! What do you bloody little tin soldiers think you're up to, putting fences across the road?'

The corporal said dangerously: 'That'll do from you. You've been told to turn round. I don't want any more lip.'

'Why don't you try turning me round?' Roger asked. His voice was thick and ugly. 'There are too many bloody useless military in this country, doing damn'all and eating good rations!'

'All right, mate,' the corporal said, 'you asked for it.' He nodded to the other two. 'Come on. We'll turn this loud-mouthed bleeder's car round for him.'

They clambered over the barrier, and advanced into the pool of brightness from the headlights.

Roger said: 'Advance the guards,' his voice sneering.

Now, suddenly, the tension caught John. The white line in the centre of the road marked off his territory from Pirrie's. The corporal and the original sentry were on that side; the third soldier was nearer to him. They walked forward, shielding their eyes from the glare.

He felt sweat start under his arms and along his legs. He brought the rifle up and tried to hold it steady. At any fraction of a second, he must crook his finger and kill this man, unknown, innocent. He had killed in the war, but never from such close range, and never a fellow-countryman. Sweat seemed to stream on his forehead; he was afraid of it blinding his eyes, but dared not risk disturbing his aim to wipe it off. Clay-pipes at a fair-ground, he thought – a clay-pipe that must be shattered, for Ann, for Mary and Davey. His throat was dry.

Roger's voice split the night again, but incisive now and sober: 'All – right!'

The first shot came before the final word, and two others followed while it was still in the air. John still stood, with his rifle aiming, as the three figures slumped into the dazzle of the road. He did not move until he saw Pirrie, having advanced from his own position, stooping over them. Then he dropped his rifle to his side, and walked on to the road himself.

Roger got out of the car. Pirrie looked up at John.

'I must apologize for poaching, partner,' he said. His voice was as cool and precise as ever. 'They were such a good lie.'

'Dead?' Roger asked.

Pirrie nodded. 'Of course.'

'Then we'll clear them into the ditch first,' Roger said. 'After that, the barrier. I don't think we're likely to be surprised, but we don't want to take chances.'

The body that John pulled away was limp and heavy. He avoided looking at the face at first. Then, in the shadow at the side of the road, he glanced at it. A lad, not more than twenty, his face young and unmarked except for the hole in one temple, gouting blood. The other two had already dropped their burdens and gone over to the barrier. They had their backs to him. He bent and kissed the unwounded side of the forehead, and eased the body down with gentleness.

It did not take them long to clear the barrier. On the other side equipment lay scattered; this, too, was thrown into the ditch. Then Roger ran back to the car, and pressed the horn button, holding it down for several seconds. Its harsh note tolled on the air like a bell.

Roger pulled the car over to the side. They waited. In a few moments they heard the sound of cars approaching. John's Vauxhall came first, closely followed by Pirrie's Ford. The Vauxhall stopped, and Ann moved over as John opened the door and got in. He pushed the accelerator pedal down hard.

Ann said: 'Where are they?'

She was looking out of the side window.

'In the ditch,' he said, as the car pulled away.

After that, for some miles, they drove in silence.

According to plan, they kept off the main roads. They finished up in a remote lane bordering a wood, near Stapleford. There, under overhanging oaks, they had cocoa from thermos flasks, with only the internal lights of one car on. Roger's Citroen was convertible into a bed, and the three women were put into that, the children being comfortable enough on the rear seats of the other two cars. The men took blankets and slept under the trees.

Pirrie put up the idea of a guard. Roger was dubious.

'I shouldn't think we'd have any trouble here. And we want

what sleep we can get. There's a long day's driving tomorrow.' He looked at John. 'What do you say, chief?'

'A night's rest – what's left of it.'

They settled down. John lay on his stomach, in the posture that Army life had taught him was most comfortable when sleeping on rough ground. He found the physical discomfort less than he had remembered it.

But sleep did not come lightly, and was broken, when it came, by meaningless dreams.

SIX

SAXON COURT stood on a small rise; the nearest approach to a hill in this part of the county. Like many similar preparatory schools, it was a converted country house, and from a distance still had elegance. A well-kept drive – its maintenance, Davey had confided, was employed as a disciplinary measure by masters and prefects – led through a brown desert that had been playing-fields to the two Georgian wings flanking a centre both earlier and uglier.

Since three cars in convoy presented a suspicious appearance, it had been decided that only John's car should go up to the school, the others being discreetly parked on the road from which the drive diverged. Steve, however, had insisted on being present when Davey was collected, and Olivia had decided to come along with him. Apart from John, there were also Ann and Mary.

The headmaster was not in his study. His study door stood open, looking out, like a vacant throne-room, on to a disordered palace. There was a traffic of small boys in the hall and up and down the main staircase; their chatter was loud and excited and, John thought, unsure. From one room leading off the hall came the murmur of Latin verbs, but there were others which yielded only uproar.

John was on the point of asking one of the boys where he might find the headmaster, when he appeared, hurrying down the stairs. He saw the small group waiting for him, and came down the last few steps more decorously.

Dr Cassop was a young headmaster, comfortably under forty, and had always seemed elegant. He retained the elegance today, but the handsome gown and neatly balanced mortar-board only served to point up the fact that he was a worried and unhappy man. He recognized John.

'Mr Custance, of course – and Mrs Custance. But I thought you lived in London? How did you get out?'

'We had been spending a few days in the country,' John said, 'with friends. This is Mrs Buckley, and her son. We've come to collect David. I should like to take him away for a little while – until things settle down.'

Dr Cassop showed none of the reluctance Miss Errington had at the thought of losing a pupil. He said eagerly:

'Oh yes. Of course. I think it's a good idea.'

'Have any other parents taken their children?' John asked.

'A couple. You see, most of them are Londoners.' He shook his head. 'I should be most relieved if it were possible to send all the boys home, and close the school for the time being. The news ...'

John nodded. They had heard, on the car radios, a guarded bulletin which spoke of some disturbances in Central London and in certain unspecified provincial cities. This information had clearly only been given as an accompaniment to the warning that any breach of public order would be put down severely.

'At least, things are quiet enough here,' John said. The din all round them increased as a classroom-door opened to release a batch of boys, presumably at the close of a lesson. 'In a noisy kind of way,' he added.

Dr Cassop took the remark neither as a joke nor as a reflection on his school's discipline. He looked round at the boys in a distracted unseeing fashion that made John realize that there was more to his strangeness than either worry or unhappiness. There was fear.

'You haven't heard any other news, I suppose?' Dr Cassop asked. 'Anything not on the radio? I have an impression ... there was no mail this morning.'

'I shouldn't think there would be any mail,' John said, 'until the situation has improved.'

'Improved?' He looked at John nakedly. 'When? How?'

John was sure of something else; it would not be long before he deserted his charges. His immediate reaction to this intuition was an angry one, but anger died as the memory rose in his mind of the quiet, bloody young face in the ditch.

He wanted only to get away. He said briefly:

'If we can take David ...'

'Yes, of course. I'll . . . Why, there he is.'

Davey had seen them simultaneously. He dashed along the corridor and hurled himself, with a cry of delight, at John.

'You will be taking David to stay with your friends?' Dr Cassop asked, ' – with Mrs Buckley, perhaps?'

John felt the boy's brown hair under his hand. There would very likely be more killings ahead; that for which he would kill was worth the killing. He looked at the headmaster.

'Our plans are not certain.' He paused. 'We mustn't detain you, Dr Cassop. I imagine you will have a lot to do – with all these boys to look after.'

The headmaster responded to the accession of brutality in John's voice. He nodded, and his fear and misery were so apparent that John saw Ann start at the perception of them.

He said: 'Yes. Of course. I hope . . . in better times. . . . Good-bye, then.'

He performed a stiff little half-bow to the ladies, and turned from them and went into his study, closing the door behind him. Davey watched him with interest.

'The fellows were saying old Cassop's got the wind-up. Do you think he has, Daddy?'

They would know, of course, and he would be aware of their knowledge. That would make things worse all round. It would not be long, John thought, before Cassop broke and made his run for it. He said to Davey:

'Maybe. So should I have, if I had a mob like you to contend with. Are you ready to leave, as you are?'

'Blimey!' Davey said, 'Mary here? Is it like end of term? Where are we going?'

Ann said: 'You must *not* say "Blimey", Davey.'

Davey said: 'Yes, Mummy. Where *are* we going? How did you get out of London – we heard about all the roads being closed. Did you fight your way through?'

'We're going up to the valley for a holiday,' John said. 'The point is – are you ready? Mary packed some of your things for you. You might as well come as you are, if you haven't any special things to get.'

'There's Spooks,' Davey said. 'Hiya, Spooks!'

Spooks proved to be a boy considerably taller than Davey; lanky of figure, with a withdrawn, rather helpless expression of face. He came up to the group and mumbled his way through Davey's hasty and excited introductions. John recalled that Spooks, whose real name was Andrew Skelton, had featured prominently in Davey's letters for some months. It was difficult to see what had drawn the two boys together, for boys do not generally seek out and befriend their opposites.

Davey said: 'Can Spooks come with us, Daddy? That would be terrific.'

'His parents might have some objection,' John said.

'Oh, no, that's all right, isn't it, Spooks? His father is in France on business, and he hasn't got a mother. She's divorced, or something. It would be all right.'

John began: 'Well...'

It was Ann who cut in sharply: 'It's quite impossible, Davey. You know very well one can't do things like that, and especially at times like this.'

Spooks stared at them silently; he looked like a child unused to hoping.

Davey said: 'But old Cassop wouldn't mind!'

'Go and get whatever you want to bring with you, Davey,' John said. 'Perhaps Spooks would like to go along and lend you a hand. Run along now.'

The two boys went off together. Mary and Steve had wandered off out of earshot.

John said: 'I think we might take him.'

Something in Ann's expression reminded him of what he had seen in the headmaster's; not the fear, but the guilt.

She said: 'No, it's ridiculous.'

'You know,' John said, 'Cassop is going to clear out. That's certain. I don't know whether any of the junior masters will stay with the boys, but if they did, it would only be postponing the evil. Whatever happens to London, this place is likely to be a wilderness in a few weeks. I don't like the idea of leaving Spooks behind when we go.'

Ann said angrily: 'Why not take the whole school with us, then?'

'Not the whole school,' John said gently. 'Just one boy – Davey's best friend here.'

Bewilderment replaced anger in her tone. 'I think I've just begun to understand what we may be in for. It may not be easy, getting to the valley. We've got two children to look after already.'

'If things do break up completely,' John said, 'some of these boys may survive it, young as they are. The Spooks kind wouldn't though. If we leave him, it's a good chance we are leaving him to die.'

'How many boys did we leave behind to die in London?' Ann asked. 'A million?'

John did not answer at once. His gaze took in the hall, invaded now by a new rush of boys from another class-room. When he turned back to Ann, he said:

'You do know what you're doing, don't you, darling? I suppose we're all changing, but in different ways.'

She said defensively: 'I shall have the children to cope with, you know, while you're being the gallant warrior with Roger and Mr Pirrie.'

'I can't insist, can I?' John asked.

Ann looked at him. 'When you told me – about Miss Errington, I thought it was dreadful. But I still hadn't realized what was happening. I do now. We've got to get to the valley, and get the children there as well. We can't afford any extras, even this boy.'

John shrugged. Davey came back, carrying a small attaché case; he had a brisk and happy look and resembled a small-scale Government official. Spooks trailed behind him.

Davey said: 'I've got the important things, like my stamp-album. I put my spare socks in, too.' He looked at his mother for approval. 'Spooks has promised to look after my mice until I get back. One of my does is pregnant, and I've told him he can sell the litter when they arrive.'

John said: 'Well, we'd better be getting along to the car.' He avoided looking at the gangling Spooks.

Olivia, who had taken no previous part in the conversation, broke her silence. She said:

'I think Spooks could come along. Would you like to come with us, Spooks?'

Ann said: 'Olivia! You know...'

Olivia said apologetically: 'I meant, in our car. We only have the one child, after all. It would only be a matter of evening things up.'

The two women stared briefly at each other. On Ann's side there was guilt again, and anger moved by that guilt. Olivia showed only shy embarrassment. Had there been the least trace of moral condescension, John thought, it would have meant a rift that the safety of the party could not afford. As it was, Ann's anger faded.

She said: 'Do as you like. Don't you think you ought to consult Roger, though?'

Davey, who had been following the interchange with interest but without understanding said:

'Is Uncle Roger here, too? I'm sure he'd like Spooks. Spooks is ferociously witty, like he is. Say something witty, Spooks.'

Spooks stared at them, in agonized helplessness. Olivia smiled at him.

'Never mind, Spooks. You would like to come with us?'

He nodded his head slowly up and down. Davey grabbed him by the arm. 'Just the job!' he exclaimed. 'Come on, Spooks, I'll go and help you pack now.' For a moment he looked thoughtful. 'What about the mice?'

'The mice,' John ordered, 'remain behind. Give them away to someone.'

Davey turned to Spooks. 'Do you think we could get sixpence each for them, off Bannister?'

John looked at Ann over their son's head; after a moment, she also smiled. John said:

'We're leaving in five minutes. That's all the time you have for Spooks's packing and your joint commercial transactions.'

The two boys prepared to turn away. Davey said thoughtfully: 'We should get a bob at least for the one that's pregnant.'

They had expected to be stopped on the roads by the military, and with that possibility in view had devised three different stories to account for the northward journeys of the three cars; the important thing, John felt, was to avoid the impression of a convoy. But in fact there was no attempt at inquisition. The considerable number of military vehicles on the roads was interspersed with private cars in a normal and mutually tolerant traffic. After leaving Saxon Court, they made for the Great North Road again, and drove northwards uneventfully throughout the morning.

In the late afternoon, they stopped for a meal in a lane, a little north of Newark. The day had been cloudy, but was now brilliantly blue and sunlit, with a mass of cloud, rolling away to the west, poised in white billows and turrets. The fields on either side of them were potato fields planted for the hopeful second crop; apart from the bareness of hedge-rows empty of grass, there was nothing to distinguish the scene from any country landscape in a thriving fruitful world.

The three boys had found a bank and were sliding down it, using for a sleigh an old panel of wood, discarded probably from some gipsy caravan years before. Mary watched them, half envious, half scornful. She had developed a lot since the hill climbing in the valley of fourteen months before.

The men, sitting in Pirrie's Ford, discussed things.

John said: 'If we can get north of Ripon today, we should be all right for the run to the valley tomorrow.'

'We could get farther than that,' Roger said.

'I suppose we could. I doubt if it would be worth it, though. The main thing is to get clear of population centres. Once we're away from the West Riding, we should be safe enough from anything that happens.'

Pirrie said: 'I am not objecting, mind you, nor regretting having joined you on this little trip, but does it not seem possible that the dangers of violence may have been over-estimated? We have had a very smooth progress. Neither Grantham nor Newark showed any signs of imminent breakdown.'

'Peterborough was sealed off,' Roger said. 'I think those towns that still have free passage are too busy congratulating themselves on being missed to begin worrying about what else may be happening. You saw those queues outside the bakeries?'

'Very orderly queues,' observed Pirrie.

'The trouble is,' said John, 'that we don't know just when Welling is going to take his drastic action. It's nearly twenty-four hours since the cities and large towns were sealed off. When the bombs drop, the whole country is going to erupt in panic. Welling hopes to be able to control things, but he won't expect to have any degree of control for the first few days. I still think that, providing we can get clear of the major centres of population by that time, we should be all right.'

'Atom bombs, and hydrogen bombs,' Pirrie said thoughtfully. 'I really wonder.'

Roger said shortly: 'I don't. I know Haggerty. He wasn't lying.'

'It is not on the score of *morality* that I find them unlikely,' said Pirrie, 'but on that of temperament. The English, being sluggish in the imagination, would find no difficulty in acquiescing in measures which – their common sense would tell them – must lead to the death by starvation of millions. But direct action – murder for self-preservation – is a different matter. I find it difficult to believe they could ever bring themselves to the sticking-point.'

'We haven't done so badly,' Roger said. He grinned. 'You, particularly.'

'My mother,' Pirrie said simply, 'was French. But you fail to take my point. I had not meant that the English are inhibited from violence. Under the right circumstances, they will murder with a will, and more cheerfully than most. But they are sluggish in logic as well as imagination. They will preserve illusions to the very end. It is only after that that they will fight like particularly savage tigers.'

'And when did you reach the end?' Roger asked.

Pirrie smiled. 'A long time ago. I came to the understanding that all men are friends by convenience and enemies by choice.'

Roger looked at him curiously. 'I follow you part of the way. There are some real ties.'

'Some alliances,' said Pirrie, 'last longer than others. But they remain alliances. Our own is a particularly valuable one.'

The women were in the Buckleys' car. Millicent now put her head out of the window, and called out to them:

'News!'

One of the two car radios was kept permanently in operation. The men walked back to see what it was.

Ann said, as they approached: 'It sounds like trouble.'

The announcer's voice was still suave, but grave as well.

' ... further emergency bulletins will be issued as they are deemed necessary, in addition to the normal news readings.

'There has been further rioting in Central London, and troops have moved in from the outskirts to control this and to maintain order. In South London, an attempt has been made by an organized mob to break through the military barriers set up yesterday following the temporary ban on travel. The situation here is confused; fresh military forces are moving up to deal with it.'

'Now that we're clear,' Roger said, 'I don't mind them having the guts to break out. Good for them.'

The announcer continued: 'There are reports of even more serious outbreaks of disorder in the North of England. Riots are reported to have occurred in several major cities, notably Liverpool, Manchester, and Leeds, and in the case of Leeds official contact has been lost.'

'Leeds!' John said. 'That's less good.'

'The Government,' the voice went on, 'has issued the following statement: "In view of disturbances in certain areas, members of the public are warned that severe counter-measures may have to be taken. There is a real danger, if mob violence were to continue, that the country might lapse into anarchy, and the Government is determined to avoid this at all costs. The duty of the individual citizen is to go about his business quietly and to cooperate with the police and military authorities who are concerned with maintaining order." That is the end of the present bulletin.'

A cinema organ began to play 'The Teddy-Bears' Picnic'; Ann switched the volume down until it was only just audible.

Roger said: 'If we drove all night, we could reach the valley by the morning. I don't like the sound of all this. It looks as though Leeds has broken loose. I think we'd better travel while the travelling's good.'

'We didn't get much sleep last night,' John said. 'A night run across Mossdale isn't a picnic at the best of times.'

'Ann and Millicent can both take a spell at the wheel,' Roger pointed out.

Ann said: 'But Olivia can't drive, can she?'

'Don't worry about me,' Roger said. 'I've brought my benzedrine with me. I can keep awake for two or three days if necessary.'

Pirrie said: 'May I suggest that we concentrate immediately on getting clear of the West Riding? When we have done that, we can decide whether to carry right on or not.'

'Yes,' John said, 'we'll do that.'

From the top of the bank, the boys called down to them, waving their arms towards the sky. Listening, they heard the hum of aircraft engines approaching. Their eyes searched the clear sky. The planes came into view over the hedge which topped the bank. They were heavy bombers, flying north, at not more than three or four thousand feet.

They watched, in a silence that seemed to shiver, until they had passed right over. They could hear the engines, and the excited chatter of the boys, but neither of these affected the sharp-edged silence of their own thoughts.

'Leeds?' Ann whispered, when they had gone.

Nobody answered at first. It was Pirrie who spoke finally, his voice as calm and precisely modulated as ever:

'Possibly. There are the other explanations, of course. But in any case, I think we ought to move, don't you?'

When they set off, Davey had joined Steve and Spooks in the Citroen, which was leading the way at this point. The Ford came second, and John's Vauxhall, carrying now only Mary and Ann in addition to himself, brought up the rear.

Doncaster was sealed off, but the detour roads had been well posted. Meshed in with an increasing military traffic, they went round to the north-east, through a series of little peaceful villages. They were in the Vale of York; the land was very flat and the villages straggling and prosperous. It was not until they had got back to the North Road that they were halted at a military checkpoint.

There was a sergeant in charge. He was a Yorkshireman, possibly a native of these parts. He looked down at Roger benevolently:

'A.1 closed except to military vehicles, sir.'

Roger asked him: 'What's the idea?'

'Trouble in Leeds. Where were you wanting to get to?'

'Westmorland.'

He shook his head, but in appreciation of their problem rather than negation. 'I should back-track on to the York road, if I was you. If you cut off just before Selby, you can go through Thorpe Willoughby to Tadcaster. I should steer well clear of Leeds though.'

Roger said: 'There are some funny rumours about.'

'I reckon there are, too,' said the sergeant.

'We saw planes flying up this way a couple of hours back,' Roger added. 'Bombing planes.'

'Yes,' the sergeant said. 'They went right over. I always feel 'appier being out in the country when things like that are up aloft. Funny, isn't it – being uneasy when your own planes go over? That lot went right over, but I should stay clear of Leeds, anyway.'

'Thanks,' Roger said, 'we will.'

The convoy reversed itself and headed back. The road by which they had come would have taken them south; instead they turned north-east and found themselves, with the military vehicles left behind, travelling deserted lanes.

Ann said: 'Our minds can't grasp it properly, can they? The news bulletins, the military check-points – they're one kind of thing. This is another. A summer evening in the country – the same country that's always been here.'

'A bit bare,' John said. He pointed to the grassless hedgerows.

'It doesn't seem enough,' Ann said, 'to account for famine, flight, murder, atom bombs . . . ' she hesitated; he glanced at her, ' . . . or refusing to take a boy with us to safety.'

John said: 'Motives are naked now. We shall have to learn to live with them.'

Ann said passionately: 'I wish we were there! I wish we could get into the valley and shut David's gate behind us.'

'Tomorrow, I hope.'

The lane they were in wound awkwardly through high-hedge country. They dropped back behind the others' cars – Pirrie's Ford, with a surprising degree of manoeuvrability, hung right on to the Citroen's heels. As the Vauxhall approached a gate-house, standing back from the road, the crossing gates slowly began to close.

Braking, John said: 'Damn! And a ten-minute wait before the train even comes in sight, if I know country crossings. I wonder if they might be persuaded to let us through for five bob.'

He slipped out of the car, and walked round it. To the right, a gap in the hedge showed the barren symmetrical range of hills which were the tip for a nearby colliery. He put his head over the gate and looked along the line. There was no sign of smoke, and the line ran straight for miles in either direction. He walked up to the gate-house, and called:

'Hello, there!'

There was no immediate reply. He called again, and this time he heard something, but too indistinct to be an answer. It was a gasping, sobbing noise, from somewhere inside the house.

The window on to the road showed him nothing. He went round on to the line, to the window that looked across it. It was easy enough to see, as he looked in, where the noise had come from. A woman lay in the middle of the floor. Her clothes were torn and there was blood on her face; one leg was doubled underneath her. About her, the room was in confusion – drawers pulled out, a wall clock splintered.

It was the first time he had seen it in England, but in Italy, during the war, he had observed not dissimilar scenes. The trail of the looter ... but here, in rural England. The casual reality of this horror in so remote a spot showed more clearly than the military check-points or the winging bombers that the break-up had come, irrevocably.

He was still looking through the window when memory gripped and tightened on him. The gates.... With the woman lying here, perhaps dying, who had closed the gates? And why? From here the road, and the car, were invisible. He turned quickly, and as he did heard Ann cry out.

He ran round the side of the gate-house. The car doors were open and a struggle was taking place inside. He could see Ann fighting with a man in front; there was another man in the back, and he could not see Mary.

He had some hope, he thought, of surprising them. The guns were in the car. He looked quickly for a weapon of some kind, and saw a piece of rough wood lying beside the porch of the gatehouse. He bent down to pick it up. As he did, he heard a man's laugh from close beside him. He straightened up again, and looked into the eyes of the man who was waiting in the shadow of the porch, just as the length of pit-prop crashed down against the side of his head.

He tried to cry out, but the words caught in his throat, and he stumbled and fell.

Someone was bathing his head. He saw first a handkerchief and saw that it was dark with clotted blood; then he looked up into Olivia's face.

She said: 'Johnny, are you better now?'

'Ann?' he said. 'Mary?'

'Lie quiet.' She called: 'Roger, he's come round.'

The crossing gates were open. The Citroen and the Ford stood in the road. The three boys were in the back of the Citroen, looking out, but shocked out of their usual chatter. Roger and the Pirries came out of the gate-house. Roger's face was grim; Pirrie's wore its customary blandness.

Roger said: 'What happened, Johnny?'

He told them. His head was aching; he had a physical urge to lie down and go to sleep.

Roger said: 'You've probably been out about half an hour. We were the other side of the Leeds road before we missed you.'

Pirrie said: 'Half an hour is, I should estimate, twenty miles for looters in this kind of country. That opens up rather a wide circle. And, of course, a widening circle. These parts are honeycombed with roads.'

Olivia was bandaging the side of his head; the pressure, gentle as it was, made the pain worse.

Roger looked down at him: 'Well, Johnny – what's it to be? It will have to be a rush decision.'

He tried to collect his rambling thoughts.

He said: 'Will you take Davey? That's the important thing. You know the way, don't you?'

Roger asked: 'And you?'

John was silent. The implications of what Pirrie had said were coming home to him. The odds were fantastically high against his finding them. And even when he did find them....

'If you could let me have a gun,' he said, ' – they got away with the guns as well.'

Roger said gently: 'Look, Johnny, you're in charge of the expedition. You're not just planning for yourself; you're planning for all of us.'

He shook his head. 'If you don't get through into the North Riding, at least tonight, you may not be able to get clear at all. I'll manage.'

Pirrie had moved a little way off; he was looking at the sky in an abstract fashion.

'Yes,' Roger said, 'you'll manage. What the hell do you think you are – a combination of Napoleon and Superman? What are you going to use for wings?'

John said: 'I don't know whether you could all crowd in the Citroen ... if you could spare me the Ford.... '

'We're travelling as a party,' Roger said. 'If you go back, you take us with you.' He paused. 'That woman's dead in there – you might as well know that.'

'Take Davey,' John said. 'That's all.'

'You damned fool!' Roger said. 'Do you think Olivia would let me carry on even if I wanted to? We'll find them. To hell with the odds.'

Pirrie looked round, blinking mildly. 'Have you reached a decision?' he inquired.

John said: 'It seems to have been reached for me. I suppose this is where the alliance ceases to be valuable, Mr Pirrie? You've got the valley marked on your road map. I'll give you a note for my brother, if you like. You can tell him we've been held up.'

'I have been examining the situation,' Pirrie said, 'If you will forgive my putting things bluntly, I am rather surprised that they should have left the scene so quickly.'

Roger said sharply: 'Why?'

Pirrie nodded towards the gatehouse. 'They spent more than half an hour there.'

John said dully: 'You mean – rape?'

'Yes. The explanation would seem to be that they guessed our three cars were together, and cut off the straggler deliberately. They would therefore be anxious to clear out of the immediate vicinity in case the other two cars should come back in search of the third.'

'Does that help us?' Roger asked.

'I think so,' Pirrie said. 'They would leave the immediate vicinity. We know they turned the car back towards the North Road because they left the gates shut against traffic. But I do not think they would go as far as the North Road without stopping again.'

'Stopping again?' John asked.

Looking at Roger's impassive face, he saw that he had taken Pirrie's meaning. Then he himself understood. He struggled to his feet.

Roger said: 'There are still some things to work out. There are well over half a dozen side roads between here and A.1. And you've got to remember that they will be listening for the noise of engines. We shall have to explore them one by one – and on foot.'

Despair climbing back on his shoulders, John said:

'By the time we've done that...'

'If we rush the cars down the first side road,' Roger said, 'it might be giving them just the chance they need to get away.'

As they walked back, in silence, to where the two cars stood, Spooks put his head out of the back of the Citroen. His voice was thin and very high-pitched. He said:

'Has someone kidnapped Davey's mother, and Mary?'

'Yes,' Roger said. 'We're going to get them back.'

'And they've taken the Vauxhall?'

Roger said: 'Yes. Keep quiet, Spooks. We've got to work things out.'

'Then we can find them easily!' Spooks said.

'Yes, we'll find them,' Roger said. He got into the driving seat, and prepared to turn the car round. John was still dazed. It was Pirrie who asked Spooks:

'Easily? How?'

Spooks pointed down the road along which they had come. 'By the oil trail.'

The three men stared at the tarmac. Trail was a high term for it, but there were spots of oil in places along the road.

'Blind!' Roger said. 'Why didn't we see that? But it might not be the Vauxhall. More likely the Ford.'

'No,' Spooks insisted. 'It must be the Vauxhall. It's left a bit bigger stain where it was standing.'

'My God!' Roger said. 'What were you at school – Chief Boy Scout?'

Spooks shook his head. 'I wasn't in the Scouts. I didn't like the camping.'

Roger said exultantly: 'We've got them! We've got the bastards! Ignore that last expression, Spooks.'

'All right,' Spooks said amiably. 'But I did know it already.'

At each junction they stopped the cars, and searched for the oil trail. It was far too inconspicuous to be seen without getting out of the cars. The third side road was on the outskirts of a village; there the trail turned right. A sign-post said: Norton 1½ m.

'I think this is our stretch,' Roger said. 'We could try blazing right along in one of the cars. If we got past them with one car, we could make a neat sandwich. I think they would be between here and the next village. They sheered off sharply enough from this one.'

'It would work,' Pirrie said thoughtfully. 'On the other hand, they would probably fight it out. They've got an automatic and a rifle and revolver in that car. It might prove difficult to get at them without hurting the women.'

'Any other ideas?'

John tried to think, but his mind was too full of sick hatred, poised between some kind of hope and despair.

Pirrie said: 'This country is very flat. If one of us were to shin up that oak, he might get a glimpse of them with the glasses.'

The oak stood in the angle of the road. Roger surveyed it carefully. 'Give me a bunk-up to the first branch, and I reckon I shall be all right.'

He climbed the tree easily; he had to go high to find a gap in the leaves to give him a view. They could barely see him from below. He called suddenly:

'Yes!'

John cried: 'Where are they?'

'About three-quarters of a mile along. Pulled into a field on the left hand side of the road. I'm coming down.'

John said: 'And Ann – and Mary?'

Roger scrambled down and dropped from the lowest branch. He avoided John's eyes.

'Yes, they're there.'

Pirrie said thoughtfully: 'On the left of the road. Are they pulled far in?'

'Clear of the opening – behind the hedge. If we went at them from the front we should be going in blind.'

Pirrie went across to the Ford. He came back with the heavy sporting rifle which was his weapon of choice.

He said: 'Three-quarters of a mile – give me ten minutes. Then take the Citroen along there fast, and pull up a few hundred yards past them. Fire a few shots – not at them, but back along the lane. I fancy that will put them into the sort of position I want.'

'Ten minutes!' John said.

'You want to get them out alive,' Pirrie said.

'They may – be ready to clear off before then.'

'You will hear them if they do. It will be noisy – backing out of a field. If you do, chase them with the Citroen and don't hesitate to let them have it.' Pirrie hesitated. 'You see, it will be unlikely that they will still have your wife and daughter with them in that case.'

And with a small indefinite nod, Pirrie started off along the road. A little way along he found a gap in the hedge, and ducked through it.

Roger looked at his watch. 'We'd better be ready,' he said. 'Olivia, Millicent – take the boys in the Ford. Come on, Johnny.'

John sat beside him in the front of the Citroen. He grinned painfully.

'I'm leading this well, aren't I?'

Roger glanced at him. 'Take it easy. You're lucky to be conscious.'

John felt his nails tighten against the seat of the car.

'Every minute . . . ' he said. 'The bloody swines! God knows, it's bad enough for Ann, but Mary . . . '

Roger repeated: 'Take it easy.' He looked at his watch again. 'With luck, our friends along the road have got just over nine minutes to live.'

The thought crossed his other thoughts, irrelevantly, surprisingly; so much that he voiced it:

'We passed a telephone box just now. Nobody thought of getting the police.'

'Why should we?' Roger said. 'There's no such thing as public safety any longer. It's all private now.' His fingernails tapped the steering-wheel. 'So is vengeance.'

Neither spoke for the remainder of the waiting time. Still without a word, Roger started the car off and accelerated rapidly through the gears. They roared at the limit of the Citroen's speed and noisiness along the narrow lane. In less than a minute, they had passed the opening to the field, and glimpsed the Vauxhall standing behind the hedge. The road ran straight for a further fifty yards. Roger braked sharply at the bend, and skidded the car across to take up the full width of the road.

John whipped open the door at his side. He had the automatic from Roger's car; leaning across the bonnet of the Citroen, he fired a short burst. The shots rattled like darts against the shield of the placid summer afternoon. Then, in the distance, there were three more shots. Silence followed them.

Roger was still in the car. John said:

'I'm going through the hedge. You'd better stay here.'

Roger nodded. The hedge was thick, but John crashed his way through it, the blackthorn spikes ripping his skin as he did so. He looked back along the field. There were bodies on the ground. From the far end of the field, Pirrie was sedately advancing, his rifle tucked neatly under his arm. Listening, John heard groans.

He began to run, his feet slipping and twisting on the ploughed ground.

Ann held Mary cradled in her lap, on the ground beside the car. They were both alive. The groans he had heard were coming from the three men who lay nearby. As John approached, one of them – small and wiry, with a narrow face covered with a stubble of ginger beard – began to get up. One arm hung loosely, but he had a revolver in the other.

John saw Pirrie lift his rifle, swiftly but without hurry. He heard the faint phutting noise of the silenced report, and the man fell, with a cry of pain. A bird which had settled on the hedge since the first disturbance, rose again and flapped away into the clear sky.

He brought rugs from the car, and covered Ann and Mary where they lay. He said, speaking in a whisper, as though even the sound of speech might hurt them further:

'Ann darling – Mary – it's all right now.'

They did not answer. Mary was sobbing quietly. Ann looked at him, and looked away.

Pirrie covered the last few yards. He kicked the man who lay nearest to him, dispassionately but with precision. The man shrieked, and then subsided again into moaning.

At that moment, Roger came through the gap from the road, revolver in hand. He examined the scene, his gaze passing quickly from the huddled woman and the girl to the three wounded men. He looked at Pirrie.

'Not as tidy a job as last time,' he observed.

'It occurred to me,' said Pirrie – his voice sounded as out of place in the calm summer countryside as did the scene of misery and blood in which he had played his part – 'that the guilty do not have the right to die as quickly as the innocent. It was a strange thought, was it not?' He stared at John. 'I believe you have the right of execution.'

One of the three men had been wounded in the thigh. He lay in a curious twisted posture, with his hands pressed against the wound. His face was crumpled, as a child's might be, in lines of misery and pain. But he had been attending to what Pirrie said. He looked at John now, with animal supplication.

John turned away. He said: 'You finish them off.'

With flat unhappy wonder, he thought: in the past, there was always due process of law. Now law itself is a casual word in a ploughed field, backed by guns.

His words had not been directed to anyone in particular. Looking down at Ann and Mary, he heard Roger's revolver crack once, and again, and heard the gasp of breath forced out by the last agony. Then Ann cried out:

'Roger!'

Roger said in a soft voice: 'Yes, Ann.'

Ann released Mary gently, and got to her feet. She clenched her teeth against pain, and John went to help her. He still had the automatic strapped on his shoulder. He tried to stop her when she reached for it, but she pulled it from him.

Two of the men were dead. The third was the one who had been wounded in the thigh. Ann limped over to stand beside him. He looked up at her, and John saw behind the twisted tormented fear of his face the beginning of hope.

He said: 'I'm sorry, Missus. I'm sorry.'

He spoke in a thick Yorkshire accent. There had been a driver, John remembered, in his old platoon in North Africa who had had that sort of voice, a cheerful fat little fellow who had been blown up just outside Bizerta.

Ann pointed the rifle. The man cried:

'No, Missus, no! I've got kids ...'

Ann's voice was flat. 'This is not because of me,' she said. 'It's because of my daughter. When you were ... I swore to myself that I would kill you if I got the chance.'

'No! You can't. It's murder!'

She found some difficulty in releasing the safety catch. He stared up at her, incredulously, while she did so, and was still staring when the bullets began tearing through his body. He shrieked once or twice, and then was quiet. She went on firing until the magazine was exhausted. There was comparative silence after that, broken only by Mary's sobbing.

Pirrie said calmly: 'That was very well done, Mrs Custance. Now you had better rest again, until we can get the car out of here.'

Roger said: 'I'll move her.'

He got in the Vauxhall, and reversed sharply. A back wheel went over the body of one of the men. He drove the car through the gap, and out on to the road. He called:

'Bring them, will you?'

John lifted his daughter and carried her out of the car. Pirrie helped to support Ann. When they were both in the car, Roger sounded the horn several times. Then he slipped out. He said to John:

'Take over. We'll get clear of here before we do anything else – just in case the shots have attracted anyone. Then Olivia can look after them.'

John pointed to the field. 'And those?'

Through the gap the three bodies were still visible, sprawled against the brown earth. Flies were beginning to settle on them.

Roger showed genuine surprise. 'What about them?'

'We aren't going to bury them?'

Pirrie chuckled drily. 'We have no time, I fear, for that corporal work of mercy.'

The Ford drove up, and Olivia got out and hurried to join Ann and Mary. Pirrie walked back to take her place at the wheel.

Roger said: 'No point in burying them. We've lost time, Johnny. Pull up just beyond Tadcaster – O.K.?'

John nodded. Pirrie called:

'I'll take over as tail-end Charlie.'

'Fair enough,' Roger said. 'Let's get moving.'

SEVEN

TADCASTER was on edge, like a border town half-frightened, half-excited, at the prospect of invasion. They filled up their tanks, and the garage proprietor looked at the money they gave him as though wondering what value it had. They got a newspaper there, too. It was a copy of the *Yorkshire Evening Press* – it was stamped 3d and they were charged 6d, without even an undertone of apology. The news it gave was identical with that which they had heard on the radio; the dull solemnity of the official hand-out barely concealed a note of fear.

They left Tadcaster and pulled into a lane, just off the main road. They had filled their vacuum flasks in the town but had to rely on their original stores of food. Mary seemed to have recovered by now; she drank tea and had a little from the tin of meat they opened. But Ann would not eat or drink anything. She sat in a silence that was unfathomable – whether of pain, shame, or brooding bitter triumph, John could not tell. He tried to get her to talk at first, but Olivia, who had stayed with them, warned him off silently.

The Citroen and the Vauxhall had been drawn up side by side, occupying the entire width of the narrow lane, and they had their meal communally in the two cars. The radio jabbered softly – a recording of a talk on Moorish architecture. It was the sort of thing that almost parodied the vaunted British phlegm. Perhaps it had been put on with that in mind; but the situation, John thought, was not so easily to be played down.

When the voice stopped, abruptly, the immediate thought was that the set had broken down. Roger nodded to John, and he switched on the radio in his own car; but nothing happened.

'Their breakdown,' Roger said. 'I feel still hungry. Think we dare risk another tin, Skipper?'

'We probably could,' John said, 'but until we get clear of the West Riding, I'd rather we didn't.'

'Fair enough,' Roger said. 'I'll move the buckle one notch to the right.'

The voice began suddenly and, with both radios now on, seemed very loud. The accent was quite unlike what might be expected on the B.B.C. – a lightly veneered Cockney. The voice was angry, and scared at the same time:

'This is the Citizens' Emergency Committee in London. We have taken charge of the B.B.C. Stand by for an emergency announcement. Stand by. We will play an interval signal until the announcement is ready. Please stand by.'

'Aha!' Roger said. 'Citizens' Emergency Committee, is it? Who the bloody hell is wasting effort on revolutions at a time like this?'

From the other car, Olivia looked at him reproachfully. He said rather loudly:

'Don't worry about the kids. It's no longer a question of Eton or Borstal. They are going to be potato-grubbers however good their table manners.'

The promised interval signal was played; the chimes, altogether incongruous, of Bow Bells. Ann looked up, and John caught her eye; those jingling changes were something that went back through their lives to childhood – for a moment, they *were* childhood and innocence in a world of plenty.

He said, only loud enough for her to hear: 'It won't always be like this.'

She looked at him indifferently. 'Won't it?'

The new voice was more typical of a broadcasting announcer. But it still held an unprofessional urgency.

'This is London. We bring you the first bulletin of the Citizens' Emergency Committee.

'The Citizens' Emergency Committee has taken over the government of London and the Home Counties owing to the unparalleled treachery of the late Prime Minister, Raymond Welling. We have incontrovertible evidence that this man, whose duty it was to protect his fellow-citizens, has made far-reaching plans for their destruction.

'The facts are these:

'The country's food position is desperate. No more grain, meat, foodstuffs of any kind, are being sent from overseas. We have nothing to eat but what we can grow out of our own soil, or fish from our own coasts. The reason for this is that the counter-virus which was bred to attack the Chung-Li grass virus has proved inadequate.

'On learning of this situation, Welling put forward a plan which was eventually approved by the Cabinet, all of whom must share responsibility for it. Welling himself became Prime Minister for the purpose of carrying it out. The plan was that British aeroplanes should drop atomic and hydrogen bombs on the country's principal cities. It was calculated that if half the country's population were murdered in this way, it might be possible to maintain a subsistence level for the rest.'

'By God!' Roger said. 'That's not the gaff they're blowing – they're blowing the top off Vesuvius.'

'The people of London,' the voice went on, 'refuse to believe that Englishmen will carry out Welling's scheme for mass-murder. We appeal to the Air Force, who in the past have defended this city against her enemies, not to dip their hands now into innocent blood. Such a crime would besmirch not only those who performed it, but their children's children for a thousand years.

'It is known that Welling and the other members of this bestial Cabinet have gone to an Air Force base. We ask the Air Force to surrender them to face the justice of the people.

'All citizens are asked to keep calm and to remain at their posts. The restrictions imposed by Welling on travel outside city boundaries have now no legal or other validity, but citizens are urged not to attempt any panic flight out of London. The Emergency Committee is making arrangements for collecting potatoes, fish, and whatever other food is available and transporting it to London, where it will be fairly rationed out. If the country only shows the Dunkirk spirit, we can pull through. Hardship must be expected, but we can pull through.'

There was a pause. The voice continued:

'Stand by for further emergency bulletins. Meanwhile we shall play you some gramophone records.'

Roger turned off his set. 'Meanwhile,' he said, 'we shall play you some gramophone records. I never believed that story of Nero and his fiddle until now.'

Millicent Pirrie said: 'It was true, then – what you said.'

'At least,' Pirrie said, 'the story has now received wide circulation. That's much the same thing, isn't it?'

'They're mad!' Roger said. 'Stark, raving, incurably mad. How Welling must be writhing.'

'I should think so,' Millicent said indignantly.

'At their inefficiency,' Roger explained. 'What a way to carry on! At my guess, the Emergency Committee's a triumvirate, and composed of a professional anarchist, a parson, and a left-wing female schoolteacher. It would take that kind of combination to show such an ignorance of elementary human behaviour.'

John said: 'They're trying to be honest about things.'

'That's what I mean,' Roger said. 'I know I speak from the exalted wisdom of an ex-Public Relations Officer, but you don't have to have had much to do with humanity in the mass to know that honesty is never advisable and frequently disastrous.'

'It will be disastrous in this case,' Pirrie said.

'Too bloody true, it will. The country faces starvation – things are in such a state that the Prime Minister decided to wipe the cities out – the Air Force would never do such a thing, but all the same we appeal to them not to – and you can leave London but we'd rather you didn't! There's only one result news like that can have: nine million people on the move – anywhere, anyhow, but *out*.'

'But the Air Force wouldn't do it,' Olivia said. 'You know they wouldn't.'

'No,' Roger said, 'I don't know. And I wasn't prepared to risk it. On the whole, I'm inclined to think not. But it doesn,t matter *now*. I wasn't willing to take a chance on human decency when it was a matter of hydrogen bombs and famine – do you seriously imagine anyone else is going to?'

Pirrie remarked thoughtfully: 'That nine million you spoke of refers to London, of course. There are a few million urban dwellers in the West Riding as well, not to mention the north-eastern industrial areas.'

'By God, yes!' Roger said. 'This will set them on the move, too. Not quite as fast as London, but fast enough.' He looked at John. 'Well, Skipper, do we drive all night?'

John said slowly: 'It's the safest thing to do. Once we get beyond Harrogate we should be all right.'

'There is the question of route,' Pirrie suggested. He spread out his own road-map and examined it, peering through the gold-rimmed spectacles which he used for close work. 'Do we skirt Harrogate to the west and travel up the Nidd valley, or do we take the main road through Ripon? We are going through Wensleydale still?'

John said: 'What do you think, Roger?'

'Theoretically, the byways are safer. All the same, I don't like the look of that road over Masham Moor.' He looked out into the swiftly dusking sky. 'Especially by night. If we can get through on the main road, it would be a good deal easier.'

'Pirrie?' John asked.

Pirrie shrugged. 'As you prefer.'

'We'll try the main road then. We'll go round Harrogate. There's a road through Starbeck and Bilton. We'd better miss Ripon, too, to be on the safe side. I'll take the lead now, and you can bring up the rear, Roger. Blast on your horn if you find yourself dropping behind for any reason.'

Roger grinned. 'I'll put a bullet through the back of Pirrie's tin Lizzy as well.'

Pirrie smiled gently. 'I shall endeavour not to set too hot a pace for you, Mr Buckley.'

The sky had remained cloudless, and as they drove to the north the stars appeared overhead. But the moon would not be up until after midnight; they drove through a landscape only briefly illuminated by the headlights of the cars. The roads were emptier than any they had met so far. The rumbling military convoys did not reappear; the earth, or tumultuous Leeds, had swallowed them up. Occasionally, in the distance, there were noises that might have been those of guns firing, but they were far away and indeterminate. John's eye strayed to the left, half expecting to see the sky burst into atomic flame, but nothing happened. Leeds lay there – Bradford, Halifax, Huddersfield, Dewsbury, Wakefield, and all the other manufacturing towns and cities of the north Midlands. It was unlikely that they lay in peace, but their agony, whatever it was, could not touch the little convoy speeding towards its refuge.

He was terribly tired, and had to rouse himself by an act of will. The women had been given the duty of keeping their husbands awake at the wheel, but Ann sat in a stiff immobility with her eyes staring into the night, saying nothing, and paying attention to nothing. He fished, one-handed, for the benzedrine pills Roger had given him, and managed to get a drink of water from a bottle to swill them down.

Occasionally, driving uphill, he looked back, to ensure that the lights of the other two cars were still following. Mary lay stretched out on the back seat, covered up with blankets and asleep. Even though brutality used towards the young, by reason of their defencelessness, provoked greater anger and greater pity, it was still true that they were resilient. Was the wind tempered to the shorn lamb? He grimaced. All the lambs were shorn now, and the wind was from the north-east, full of ice and black frost.

They skirted Harrogate and Ripon easily enough; their lights showed that they still had electricity supplies and gave them a comforting civilized look from a distance. Things might not be too bad there yet, either. He wondered: could it all be a bad dream, from which they would awaken to find the old world reborn, that everyday world which already had begun to wear the magic of the irretrievably lost? There will be legends, he thought, of broad avenues celestially lit, of the hurrying millions who lived together without plotting each other's death, of railway trains and aeroplanes and motor-cars, of food in all its diversity. Most of all, perhaps, of policemen – custodians, without anger or malice, of a law that stretched to the ends of the earth.

He knew Masham as a small market town on the banks of the Ure. The road curved sharply just beyond the river, and he slowed down for the bend.

The block had been well sited – far enough round the bend to be invisible from the other side, but near enough to prevent a car getting up any speed again. The road was not wide enough to permit a turn. He had to brake to stop, and before he could put the car into reverse he found a rifle pointing in at his side window. A stocky man in tweeds was holding it. He said to John:

'All right, then. Come on out.'

John said: 'What's the idea?'

The man stepped back as Pirrie's Ford swept round in its turn, but he kept the rifle steady on the Vauxhall. There were others, John saw, behind him. They covered the Ford and finally the Citroen when it, too, came to a halt in front of the block.

The man in tweeds said: 'What's this – a convoy? Any more of you?'

He had a jovial Yorkshire voice; the inflection did not seem at all threatening.

John pushed the door open. 'We're travelling west,' he said, 'across the moors. My brother's a farmer in Westmorland. We're heading for his place.'

'Where are you heading from, mister?' another voice asked.

'London.'

'You got out quick, did you?' The man laughed. 'Not a very 'ealthy place just now, London, I don't reckon.'

Roger and Pirrie had both alighted – John was relieved to see that they had left their arms in the cars. Roger pointed to the road-block.

'What's the idea of the tank trap?' he asked. 'Getting ready for an invasion?'

The man in tweeds said: 'That's clever.' His voice had a note of approval. 'You've got it in one. When they come tearing up from the West Riding, the way you've done, they're not going to find it so easy to pillage this little town.'

'I get your point,' Roger said.

There was something artificial about the situation. John was able to see more clearly now; there were more than a dozen men in the road, watching them.

He said: 'We might as well get things straight. Do I take it you want us to back-track and find a road round the town? It's a nuisance, but I see your point.'

Another of the men laughed. 'Not yet you don't, mister!'

John made no reply. For a moment he weighed the possibilities of their getting back into the cars and fighting it out. But even if they were to succeed in getting back, the women and children would be in the line of fire. He waited.

It was fairly clear that the man in tweeds was the leader. One of the small Napoleons the new chaos would throw up; it was their bad luck that Masham had thrown him up so promptly. It had not been unreasonable to hope for another twelve hours' grace.

'You see,' the man in tweeds said, 'you've got to look at it from our point of view. If we didn't protect ourselves, a place like this would be buried in the first rush. I'm telling you so you will understand we're not doing anything that's not sensible and necessary. You see, as well as being a target, you might say we're a honeypot. All the flies – trying to get away from the famine and the atom bombs – they'll all be travelling along the main roads. We catch them, and then we live on them – that's the idea.'

'Bit early for cannibalism,' Roger commented. 'Or is it a habit to eat human flesh in these parts?'

The man in tweeds laughed. 'Glad to see you've got a sense of humour. All's not lost while we can find something to laugh at, eh? It's not their flesh we want – not yet, anyway. But most of 'em will be carrying something, if it's only half a bar of chocolate. You might say this is a toll-gate combined with a customs house. We inspect the luggage, and take what we want.'

John said sharply: 'Do you let us through after that?'

'Well, not through, like. But round, anyway.' His eyes – small and intent in a square well-fleshed face – fastened on John's. 'You can see what it looks like from our point of view, can't you?'

'I should say it looks like theft,' John said, 'from any point of view.'

'Ay,' the man said, 'maybe as it does. If you've travelled all the way up here from London with nought worse than theft to your names, you've been luckier than the next lot will be. All right, mister. Ask the women to bring the kids out. We'll do the searching. Come on, now. Soonest out, soonest ended.'

John glanced at the other two; he read anger in Roger's face, but acquiescence. Pirrie looked his usual polite and blank self.

'O.K.,' John said. 'Ann, you will have to wake Mary, I'm afraid. Bring her out for a moment.'

They huddled together while some of the men began ransacking the insides of the cars and the boots. They were not long in unearthing the weapons. A little man with a stubble of beard held up John's automatic rifle with a cry.

The man in tweeds said: 'Guns, eh? That's a better haul than we expected for our first.'

John said: 'There are revolvers as well. I hope you will leave us those.'

'Have some sense,' the man said. 'We're the ones who've got a town to defend.' He called to the searching men. 'Stack all the arms over here.'

'Just what do you propose to take off us?' John asked.

'That's easy enough. The guns, for a start. Apart from that, food, as I said. And petrol, of course.'

'Why petrol?'

'Because we may need it, if only for our internal lines of communication.' He grinned. 'Sounds very military, doesn't it? Bit like the old days, in some ways. But it's on our own doorsteps now.'

John said: 'We've got another eighty or ninety miles to do. The Ford can do forty to the gallon, the other two around thirty. All the tanks are pretty full. Will you leave us nine gallons between us?'

The man in tweeds said nothing. He grinned.

John looked at him. 'We'll ditch one of the big cars. Will you leave us six gallons?'

'Six gallons,' the man in tweeds said 'or one revolver – the sort of thing that might make the difference between our holding this town and seeing it go up in flames. Mister, we're not leaving you anything that we can possibly make good use of.'

'One car,' John said, 'and three gallons. So you don't have three women and four children on your consciences.'

'Nay,' the man said, 'it's all very well talking about consciences, but we've got our own women and kids to think about.'

Roger and Pirrie were standing by him. Roger said:

'They'll take your town, and they'll burn it. I hope you live just long enough to see it.'

The man stared at him. 'You don't want to start spoiling things, mister. We've been treating you fair enough, but we could turn nasty if we wanted to.'

Roger was on the verge of saying something else. John said:

'All right. That's enough, Rodge.' To the man in tweeds, he went on: 'We'll make you a present of the cars. Can we take our families through the town towards Wensley? And do you think we could have a couple of old perambulators you've finished with?'

'I'm glad to see you're more polite than your friend, but it's no – to both. No one's coming into this town. We've got our roads to guard, and the men who aren't guarding them have got work to do and sleep to get. We can't spare anyone to watch you, and it's damn certain we're not letting you go through the town unwatched.'

John looked at Roger again, and checked him. Pirrie spoke:

'Perhaps you will tell us what we can do. And what we can take – blankets?'

'Ay, we're well enough supplied with blankets.'

'And our maps?'

One of the searchers came up and reported to him:

'Reckon we've got everything worth having, Mr Spruce. Food and stuff. And the guns. Willie's syphoning the petrol.'

'In that case,' Mr Spruce said, 'you can go and help yourselves to what you want. I shouldn't carry too much, if I were you. You won't find the going so easy. If you follow the river round' – he pointed to the right – 'it's your best way for getting round the town.'

'Thank you,' Roger said. 'You're a great help.'

Mr Spruce regarded him with beady benevolence. 'You're lucky – getting here before the rush, like. We shan't have time to gossip with 'em once they start coming in fast.'

'You've got a great deal of confidence,' John said. 'But it isn't going to be as easy as you think it is.'

'I read somewhere once,' Mr Spruce said, 'how the Saxons laughed and chatted together before the Battle of Hastings.

That was when they'd just had one big battle and were getting ready for the next.'

'They lost that one,' John said. 'The Normans won.'

'Maybe they did. But it was a couple of hundred years before they travelled easy in these parts. Good luck, mister.'

John looked at the cars, stripped already of food and weapons and with Willy, a youth lean and gangling and intent, completing the syphoning of the petrol.

'May you have the same luck,' he said.

John said: 'The important thing is to get away from here. After that we can decide the best plan to follow. As far as our things are concerned, I suggest we take three small cases for the present. Rucksacks would have been better, but we haven't got them. I shouldn't bother with blankets. Fortunately, it's summer. If it's chilly, we shall have to huddle together for warmth.'

'I shall take my blanket roll,' Pirrie said.

'I don't advise it,' John told him.

Pirrie smiled, but made no reply.

The Masham men, having removed their booty, had faded back into the shadows that lined the road, and were watching them with impassive disinterest. The children, sleepy-eyed and unsteady, watched also as their elders sorted out what they needed from what had been left. John realized that he no longer counted Mary as one of the children; she was helping Ann.

They got away at last. Looking back, John saw that the Masham men were pulling the abandoned cars round to reinforce the barrier they had already set up. He wondered what would happen when the cars really began to pile up there – probably they would shove them into the river.

They toiled up rising ground, until they could look down, from a bare field, on the starlit roofs of the town lying between them and the moors. The night was very quiet.

'We'll rest here for a while,' John said. 'We can consider our plans.'

Pirrie dropped the blanket roll; he had been carrying it, at first awkwardly under his arm and then more sensibly balanced on his shoulder.

'In that case, I can get rid of these blankets,' he said.

Roger said: 'I wondered how long it would be before you realized you were carrying dead weight.'

Pirrie was busy undoing the string that tied the roll; it was arranged in a series of complicated knots. He said:

'Those people down there ... excellent surface efficiency, but I suspect the minor details are going to trip them up. I rather think the man who went through my car wasn't even carrying a knife. If he was, then his negligence is quite inexcusable.'

Roger asked curiously: 'What have you got in there?'

Pirrie looked up. In the dim starlight, he appeared to be blinking. 'When I was considerably younger,' he said, 'I used to travel in the Middle East – Trans-Jordan, Iraq, Saudi Arabia. I was looking for minerals – without much success, I must add. I learned the trick there of hiding a rifle in a blanket roll. The Arabs stole everything, but they preferred rifles.'

Pirrie completed his unravelling. From the middle of the blankets, he drew out his sporting rifle; the telescopic sight was still attached.

Roger laughed, loudly and suddenly. 'Well, I'm damned! Things don't look quite so bad after all. Good old Pirrie.'

Pirrie lifted out a small box in addition. 'Only a couple of dozen rounds, unfortunately,' he said, 'but it's better than nothing.'

'I should say it is,' said Roger. 'If we can't find a farmhouse with a car and petrol, we don't deserve to get away with it. A gun makes the difference.'

John said: 'No. No more cars.'

There was a moment's silence. Then Roger said:

'You're not starting to develop scruples, are you, Johnny? Because if you are, then the best thing you can do with Pirrie's rifle is shoot yourself. I didn't like the way those bastards down there treated us, but I have to admit they had the right idea. It's force that counts now. Anybody who doesn't understand that has got as much chance as a rabbit in a cage full of ferrets.'

Only this morning, John thought, his reasons might have been based on scruples; and along with those scruples would have gone uncertainty and reluctance to impose his own decision on the others. Now he said sharply:

'We're not taking another car, because cars are too dangerous now. We were lucky down there. They could easily have riddled us with bullets first and stripped the cars afterwards. They will have to do that eventually. If we try to make it to the valley by car, we're asking for something like that to happen. In a car, you're always in a potential ambush.'

'Reasonable,' Pirrie murmured. 'Very reasonable.'

'Eighty odd miles,' Roger said. 'On foot? You weren't expecting to find horses, were you?'

John gazed at the weed-chequered ground on which they stood; it looked as though it might once have been pasture.

'No. We're going to have to do it on foot. Probably it means three days, instead of a few hours. But if we do it slowly, it's odds on our making it. The other way, it's odds against.'

Roger said: 'I'm for getting hold of a car, and making a run for it. There's a chance we shan't meet any trouble at all; there won't be many towns will have organized as quickly as Masham did – there won't be many that will have the sense to organize anyway. If we're making a trek across country with the kids, we're bound to have trouble.'

'That's what we're going to do, though,' John said.

Roger asked: 'What do you think, Pirrie?'

'It doesn't matter what he thinks,' John said. 'I've told you what we're going to do.'

Roger nodded at the silent watchful figure of Pirrie. 'He's got the gun,' he said.

John said: 'That means he can take over running the show, if he has the inclination. But until he does, I make the decisions.' He glanced at Pirrie. 'Well?'

'Admirably put,' Pirrie remarked. 'Am I allowed to keep the rifle? I hardly think I am being particularly vain in pointing out that I happen to have the greatest degree of skill in its use. And I am not likely to develop ambitions towards leadership. You will have to take that on trust, of course.'

John said: 'Of course you keep the rifle.'

Roger said: 'So democracy's out. That's something I ought to have realized for myself. Where do we go from here?'

'Nowhere until the morning,' John said. 'In the first place, we all need a night's sleep; and in the second, there's no sense in stumbling about in the dark in country we don't know. Everybody stands an hour's watch. I'll take first; then you, Roger, Pirrie, Millicent, Olivia' – he hesitated – 'and Ann. Six hours will be as much as we can afford. Then we shall go and look for breakfast.'

The air was warm, with hardly any breeze.

'Once again,' Roger said, 'thank God it's not winter.' He called to the three boys: 'Come on, you lot. You can snuggle round me and keep me cosy.'

The field lay just under the crest of a hill. John sat above the little group of reclining figures, and looked over them to the vista of moorland that stretched away westwards. The moon would soon be up; already its radiance had begun to reinforce the starlight.

The question of whether the weather held fair would make a lot of difference to them. How easy it would be, he thought, to pray – to sacrifice, even – to the moorland gods, in the hope of turning away their wrath. He glanced at where the three boys lay curled up between Roger and Olivia. They would come to it, perhaps, or their children.

And thinking that, he felt a great weariness of spirit, as though out of the past his old self, his civilized self, challenged him to an accounting. When it sank below a certain level, was life itself worth the having any longer? They had lived in a world of morality whose lineage could be traced back nearly four thousand years. In a day, it had been swept from under them.

But were there some who still held on, still speaking the grammar of love while Babel rose all round them? If they did, he thought, they must die, and their children with them – as their predecessors had died, long ago, in the Roman arenas. For a moment, he thought that he would be glad to have the faith to die like that, but then he looked again at the little sleeping group whose head he now was, and knew their lives meant more to him than their deaths ever could.

He stood up, and walked quietly to where Ann lay with Mary

in her arms. Mary was asleep, but in the growing moonlight he could see that Ann's eyes were open.

He called softly to her: 'Ann!'

She made no reply. She did not even look up. After a time he walked away again and took up his old position.

There were some who would choose to die well rather than to live. He was sure of that, and the assurance comforted him.

EIGHT

DURING her watch, Millicent had seen distant flashes towards the south, twice or three times, and had heard a rumble of noise long afterwards. They might have been atom-bomb explosions. The question seemed irrelevant. It was unlikely that they would ever know the full story of whatever was taking place in the thickly populated parts of the country; and, in any case, it no longer interested them.

They began their march on a bright morning; it was cool but promised heat. The objective John had set them was a crossing of the northern part of Masham Moor into Coverdale. After that, they would take a minor road across Carlton Moor and then strike north to Wensleydale and the pass into Westmorland. They found a farm-house not very far away from where they had slept, and Roger wanted to raid it for food. John vetoed the idea, on the grounds that it was too near Masham. It was uncertain how far the Mashamites proposed to protect their outlying districts. The sound of shots might easily bring a protecting party up from the town.

They therefore kept away from habitation, travelling in the bare fields and keeping close beside the hedges or stone walls which formed the boundaries. It was about half-past six when they crossed the main road north of Masham, and the sun had warmed the air. The boys were happy enough, and had to be restrained from unnecessary running about. The whole party had something of a picnic air, except that Ann remained quiet, withdrawn, and unhappy.

Millicent commented on this to John, when he found himself walking beside her across a patch of broken stony ground.

She said: 'Ann shouldn't take things too much to heart, Johnny. It's all in a day's work.'

John glanced at her. Neatness was a predominating characteristic of Millicent, and she looked now as though she were out for an ordinary country walk. Pirrie, with the rifle under his arm, was about fifteen yards ahead of them.

'I don't think it's so much what happened,' John said, 'as what she did afterwards that's worrying her.'

'That's what I meant was all in a day's work,' Millicent said. She looked at John with frank admiration. 'I liked the way you handled things last night. You know – quiet, but no nonsense. I like a man to know what he wants and go and get it.'

Discounting her face, John thought, she looked a good deal more than a score of years younger than Pirrie; she was slim and tautly figured. She caught his glance, and smiled at him. He recognized something in the smile, and was shocked by it.

He said briefly: 'Someone has to make decisions.'

'At first, I didn't think you would be the kind who would, properly. Then last night I could see I was wrong about you.'

It was not, he decided, the concupiscence which shocked him in itself, but its presence in this context. Pirrie, he was sure, must have been a cuckold for some time, but that had been in London, in that warren of swarming humanity where the indulgence of one more lust could have no real importance. But here, where their interdependence was as starkly evident as the barren lines of what had been the moors, it mattered a great deal. There might yet be a morality in which the leader of the group took his women as he wished. But the old ways of winks and nudges and innuendoes were as dead as business conferences and evenings at the theatre – as dead and as impossible of resurrection. The fact that he was shocked by Millicent's failure to realize it was evidence of how deeply the realization had sunk into and conditioned his own mind.

He said, more sharply still: 'Go and take over that case from Olivia. She's had it long enough.'

She raised her eyebrows slightly. 'Just as you say, Big Chief. Whatever you say goes.'

On the edge of Witton Moor they found what John had been looking for – a small farm-house, compact and isolated. It stood on a slight rise, surrounded by potato fields. There was smoke rising from the chimney. For a moment that puzzled him, until he remembered that, in a remote spot like this, they would probably need a coal fire, even in summer, for cooking. He gave Pirrie his instructions. Pirrie nodded, and rubbed three fingers of his right hand along his nose; he had made the same gesture, John remembered now, before going out after the gang who had taken Ann and Mary.

With Roger, John walked up to the farm-house. They made no attempt at concealment, and strolled casually as though motivated by idle curiosity. John saw a curtain in one of the front windows twitch, but there was no other sign that they had been observed. An old dog sunned himself against the side of the house. Pebbles crunched under their feet, a casual and friendly sound.

There was a knocker on the door, shaped like a ram's head. John lifted it and dropped it again heavily; it clanged dully against its metal base. As they heard the tread of feet on the other side, the two men stepped a little to the right.

The door swung open. The man on the other side had to come fully into the threshold to see them properly. He was a big man; his eyes were small and cold in a weathered red face. John saw with satisfaction that he was carrying a shot-gun.

He said: 'Well, what is it you want? We've nought to sell, if it's food you're after.'

He was still too far inside the house.

John said: 'Thanks. We're not short of food, though. We've got something we think might interest you.'

'Keep it,' the man said. 'Keep it, and clear off.'

'In that case ...' John said.

He jumped inwards so that he was pressed against the wall to the right of the door, out of sight of the farmer. The man reacted immediately. 'If you want gunshot ...' he said. He came through the doorway, the gun ready, his finger on the trigger.

There was a distant crack, and at the same time the massive body turned inwards, like a top pulled by its string, and slumped towards them. As he fell, a finger contracted. The gun went off crashingly, its charge exploding against the wall of the farm-house. The echoes seemed to splinter against the calm sky. The old dog roused and barked, feebly, against the sun. A voice cried something from inside the house, and then there was silence.

John pulled the shot-gun away from under the body which

lay over it. One barrel was still unfired. With a nod to Roger, he stepped over the dead or dying man and into the house. The door opened immediately into a big living-room. The light was dimmer and John's gaze went first to the closed doors leading off the room and then to the empty staircase that ascended in one corner. Several seconds elapsed before he saw the woman who stood in the shadows by the side of the staircase.

She was quite tall, but as spare as the farmer had been broad. She was looking directly at them, and she was holding another gun. Roger saw her at the same time. He cried:

'Watch it, Johnny!'

Her hand moved along the side of the gun, but as it did so, John's own hand moved also. The clap of sound was even more deafening in the confinement of the room. She stayed upright for a moment and then, clutching at the banister to her left, crumpled up. She began to scream as she reached the ground, and went on screaming in a high strangled voice.

Roger said: 'Oh, my God!'

John said: 'Don't stand there. Get a move on. Get that other gun and let's get this house searched. We've been lucky twice but we don't have to be a third time.'

He watched while Roger reluctantly pulled the gun away from the woman; she gave no sign, but went on screaming.

Roger said: 'Her face ... '

'You take the ground floor,' John told him. 'I'll go upstairs.'

He searched quickly through the upper story, kicking doors open. He did not realize until he had nearly finished his search that he had forgotten something – that had been the second barrel and, until the shot-gun was reloaded, he was virtually weaponless. One door remained. He hesitated and then kicked this open in turn.

It was a small bedroom. A girl in her middle 'teens was sitting up in bed. She stared at him with terrified eyes.

He said to her: 'Stay here. Understand? You won't get hurt if you stay in here.'

'The guns ... ' she said. 'Ma and Pa – what was the shooting? They're not ... '

He said coldly: 'Don't move outside this room.'

There was a key in the lock. He went out, closed the door and locked it. The woman downstairs was still screaming, but less harshly than she had been. Roger stood above her, staring down.

John said, 'Well?'

Roger looked up slowly. 'It's all right. There's no one else down here.' He gazed down at the woman again. 'Breakfast cooking on the range.'

Pirrie came quietly through the open door. He lowered his rifle as he viewed the scene.

'Mission accomplished,' he commented. 'She had a gun as well? Are there any others in the house?'

'Guns or people?' John asked. 'I didn't see any other guns, did you, Rodge?'

Still looking at the woman, Roger said: 'No.'

'There's a girl upstairs,' John said. 'Daughter. I locked her in.'

'And this?' Pirrie directed the toe of one shoe towards the woman, now groaning deep-throatedly.

'She got the blast ... in the face mostly,' Roger said. 'From a couple of yards range.'

'In that case ... ' said Pirrie. He tapped the side of his rifle and looked at John. 'Do you agree?'

Roger looked at them both. John nodded. Pirrie walked with his usual precise gait to where the woman lay. As he pointed the rifle, he said: 'A revolver is so much more convenient for this sort of thing.' The rifle cracked, and the woman stopped moaning. 'In addition to which, I do not like using the ammunition for this unnecessarily. We are not likely to replace it. Shot-guns are much more likely equipment in parts like these.'

John said: 'Not a bad exchange – two shot-guns and, presumably, ammunition, for two rounds.'

Pirrie smiled. 'You will forgive me for regarding two rounds from this as worth half a dozen shot-guns. Still, it hasn't been too bad. Shall we call the others up now?'

'Yes,' John said, 'I think we might as well.'

In a strained voice, Roger said: 'Wouldn't it be better to get these bodies out of the way first – before the children come up here?'

John nodded. 'I suppose it would.' He stepped across the

corpse. 'There's generally a hole under the stairs. Yes, I thought so. In here. Wait a minute – here are the cartridges for the shotguns. Get these out first.' He peered into the dark recesses of the cubby-hole. 'I don't think there's anything else we want. You can lift her in now.'

It took all three of them to carry the dead farmer in from the door and wedge his body also into the cupboard under the stairs. Then John went out in front of the house, and waved. The day was as bright, and seemed fresher than ever with the absence of the pungent smell of powder. The old dog had settled again in its place; he saw now that it was very old indeed, and possibly blind. A watchdog that still lived when it could no longer guard was an aimless thing; but no more aimless, he thought, than the blind millions of whom they themselves were the forerunners. He let the gun drop. At any rate, it was not worth the expenditure of a cartridge.

The women came up the hill with the children. The picnic air was gone; the boys walked quietly and without saying anything. Davey came up to John. He said, in a low voice:

'What was the shooting, Daddy?'

John looked into his son's eyes. 'We have to fight for things now,' he said. 'We have to fight to live. It's something you'll have to learn.'

'Did you kill them?'

'Yes.'

'Where did you put the bodies?'

'Out of the way. Come on in. We're going to have breakfast.'

There was a stain of blood at the door, and another where the woman had lain. Davey looked at them, but he did not say anything else.

When they were all in the living-room, John said:

'We don't want to be here long. The women can be getting us a meal. There are eggs in the kitchen, and a side of bacon. Get it done quickly. Roger and Pirrie and I will be sorting out what we want to take with us.'

Spooks asked: 'Can we help you?'

'No. You boys stay here and rest yourselves. We've got a long day in front of us.'

Olivia had been staring, as Davey had done, at the marks of blood on the floor. She said:

'Were there only – the two of them?'

John said curtly: 'There's a girl upstairs – daughter. I've locked her in.'

Olivia made a move towards the stairs. 'She must be terrified!'

John's look stopped her. He said: 'I've told you – we haven't time to waste on inessentials. See to the things we need. Never mind anything else.'

For a moment she hesitated, and then she went through to the kitchen. Millicent followed her. Ann stood by the door with Mary. She said:

'Two are enough. We're going to stay outside. I don't like the smell in here.'

John nodded. 'Just as you want. You can eat out there as well, if you like.'

Ann did ot say anything, but led Mary out into the sunshine. Spooks, after a brief hesitation, followed them. The other two boys sat on the old-fashioned sofa under the window. There was a clock ticking rhythmically on the wall facing them. It was glass-fronted, so that its works were visible. They sat and stared at it, and spoke to each other in whispers.

By the time the food was ready, the men had got all they needed. They had found two large rucksacks and a smaller one, and had packed them with chunks of ham and pork and salted beef, along with some home-made bread. The cartridges for the guns were slipped in on top. They had also found an old army water-bottle. Roger suggested filling more bottles with water, but John opposed it. They would be travelling through tolerably well-watered country, and had enough to carry as it was.

When they had finished their meal, Olivia started collecting the plates together. It was when Millicent laughed that John saw what she was doing. She put the plates down again in some confusion.

John said: 'No washing up. We get moving straight away. It's an isolated place, but any house is a potential trap.'

The men began picking up their guns and rucksacks.

Olivia said: 'What about the girl?'

John glanced at her. 'What about her?'

'We can't leave her – like this.'

'If it bothers you,' John said, 'you can go and unlock her door. Tell her she can come out when she likes. It doesn't matter now.'

'But we can't leave her in the house!' She gestured towards the cupboard beneath the stairs. 'With those.'

'What do you suggest, then?'

'We could take her with us.'

John said: 'Don't be silly, Olivia. You know we can't.'

Olivia stared at him. Behind her plump diffidence, he saw, there was resolution. Thinking of her and of Roger, he reflected that crises were always likely to produce strange results in terms of human behaviour.

Olivia said: 'If not, I shall stay here with her.'

'And Roger?' John asked. 'And Steve?'

Roger said slowly: 'If Olivia wants to stay, we'll stay here with her. You don't need us, do you?'

John said: 'And when the next visitor calls, who's going to open the door? You or Olivia – or Steve?'

There was a silence. The clock ticked, marking the passing seconds of a summer morning.

Roger said then: 'Why can't we take the girl, if Olivia wants to? We brought Spooks. A girl couldn't be any danger to us, surely?'

Impatient and angry, John said: 'What makes you think she would come with us? We've just killed her parents.'

'I think she would come,' Olivia said.

'How long would you like to have to persuade her?' John asked. 'A fortnight?'

Olivia and Roger exchanged glances. Roger said:

'The rest of you go on. We'll try and catch up with you – with the girl, if she will come.'

To Roger, John said: 'You surprise me, Rodge. Surely I don't have to point out to you just how damn silly it is to split our forces now?'

They did not answer him. Pirrie and Millicent and the boys were watching in silence. John glanced at his watch.

'Look,' he said, 'I'll give you three minutes, Olivia, to talk to the girl. If she wants to come, she can. But we aren't going to waste any more time persuading her – none of us. All right?' Olivia nodded. 'I'll come up with you.'

He led the way up the stairs, unlocked the door, and pushed it open. The girl was out of bed; she looked up from a kneeling posture, possibly one of prayer. John stood aside to let Olivia enter the room. The girl stared at them both, her face expressionless.

Olivia said: 'We should like you to come with us, my dear. We are going to a safe place up in the hills. It wouldn't be safe for you to stay here.'

The girl said: 'My mother – I heard her screaming, and then she stopped.'

'She's dead,' Olivia said. 'Your father, too. There's nothing to stay here for.'

'You killed them,' the girl said. She looked at John. 'He killed them.'

Olivia said: 'Yes. They had food and we didn't. People fight over food now. We won, and they lost. It's something that can't be helped. I want you to come with us, all the same.'

The girl turned away, her face pressed against the bed clothes. In a muffled voice, she said:

'Leave me alone. Go away and leave me alone.'

John looked at Olivia and shook his head. She went over and knelt beside the girl, putting an arm round her shoulders. She said gently:

'We aren't bad people. We're just trying to save ourselves and our children, and so the men kill now, if they have to. There will be others coming who will be worse – who will kill for the sake of killing, and torture, too, perhaps.'

The girl repeated: 'Leave me alone.'

'We aren't far ahead of the mobs,' Olivia said. 'They will be coming up from the towns, looking for food. A place of this kind will draw them like flies. Your father and mother would have died, anyway, in the next few days, and you with them. Don't you believe that?'

'Go away,' the girl said. She did not look up.

John said: 'I told you, Olivia. We can't take her away against her will. And as for your staying with her – you've just said yourself the place is a death-trap.'

Olivia got up from her knees, as though acquiescing. But instead she took the girl by the shoulders and twisted her round to face her. She had considerable strength of arm, and she used it now, not brutally but with determination.

She said: 'Listen to me! You're afraid, aren't you? Aren't you?'

Her eyes held the girl as though in fascination. The girl's head nodded.

'Do you believe I want to help you?' Olivia asked her.

Again she nodded.

'You're coming with us,' Olivia said. 'We're going across the Pennines, to a place in Westmorland where we can all be quite safe, and where there won't be any more killing and brutality.' Olivia's normal reserve was entirely gone; she spoke with a bitter anger that carried conviction. 'And you are coming with us. We killed your father and mother, but if we save you we shall have made up to them a little bit. They wouldn't want you to die as they have done.'

The girl stared silently. Olivia said to John:

'You can wait outside. I'll help her dress. We shall only be a couple of minutes.'

John shrugged. 'I'll go downstairs and see that everything's ready. A couple of minutes, remember.'

'We'll be down,' Olivia said.

In the living-room, John found Roger fiddling with the controls of a radio that stood on the sideboard. He looked up as John came down the stairs.

'Nothing,' he said. 'I've tried North, Scotland, Midland, London – nothing at all.'

'Ireland?' John asked.

'Nothing I can hear. I doubt if you could pick them up from here anyway.'

'Perhaps the set's dead.'

'I found one station. I don't know what the language was – it sounded Middle European. Sounded pretty desperate, too.'

'Short waves?'

'Haven't tried.'

'I'll have a go.' Roger stood aside, and John switched down to the short wave band, and began to fan the dial, slowly and carefully. He covered three-quarters of the dial without finding anything; then he picked up a voice, distorted by crackle and fading, but speaking English. He tuned it in to its maximum, and gave it all the volume he could:

'... fragmentary, but all the evidence indicates that Western Europe has ceased to exist as a part of the civilized world.'

The accent was American. John said softly:

'So that beautiful banner yet waves.'

'Numbers of airplanes,' the voice continued, 'have been arriving during last evening in parts of the United States and Canada. By the President's order, the people in them have been given sanctuary. The President of France and senior members of the French Government, and the Dutch and Belgian Royal families are amongst those who have entered this country. It is reported from Halifax, Nova Scotia, that the British Royal family and Government have arrived there safely. According to the same report, the last Prime Minister of Great Britain, Raymond Welling, has said that the startling speed of the breakdown which has taken place there was largely due to the spread of rumours that major population centres were to be atom-bombed as a means of saving the rest of the country. These rumours, Welling claims, were entirely unfounded, but caused panic nevertheless. When told that the Atomic Energy Commission here had reported atomic-bomb explosions as occurring in Europe during the past few hours, Welling stated that he could not account for them, but thought it possible that isolated Air Force elements might have used such desperate measures in the hope of regaining control.'

Roger said: 'So it got out of hand, and he threw it up and ran.'

'One of the unsolved mysteries,' John said.

The voice went on: 'The following statement, signed by the President, was issued in Washington at nine p.m.

'It is to be expected that this country will mourn the loss to barbarism of Europe, the cradle of our Western civilization. We cannot help being grieved and shocked by what is taking place on the other side of the Atlantic Ocean. At the same time, this does not mean that there is the slightest danger of a similar catastrophe occurring here. Our food-stocks are high, and though it is probable that rations will have to be reduced in the coming months, there will be ample food for all. In the fullness of time, we shall defeat the Chung-Li virus and go out to reclaim the wide world that once we knew. Until then, our duty is to preserve within the limits of our own nation the heritage of man's greatness.'

John said bitterly: 'That's encouraging, anyway.'

He turned to see Olivia coming down the stairs with the girl. Now that she was dressed, he saw that she was two or three years older than Mary, a country girl, more distinguished by health than good looks. She looked from John's face to the stains on the floor, and back again; but her face did not show anything.

Olivia said: 'This is Jane. She's coming with us. We're all ready now, Johnny.'

John said: 'Good. Then we'll push off.'

The girl turned to Olivia. 'Before I go – could I see them, just the once?'

Olivia looked uncertain. John thought of the two bodies, crammed in, without ceremony or compunction, beneath the stairs on which the girl now stood.

He said sharply: 'No. It wouldn't do you or them any good, and we haven't got the time.'

He thought she might protest, but when Olivia urged her forward gently, she came. She looked once round the living-room, and walked out into the open.

'O.K.' John said, 'we're off.'

'One minor item,' Pirrie said. The voice on the radio was still talking, falling towards and away from them on periodic swells of volume. It was outlining some new regulation against food hoarding. Pirrie walked over to the sideboard and, in a single movement, swept the radio on to the wooden floor. It fell with a splintering of glass. With deliberate movements, Pirrie kicked it until the cabinet was shattered and the broken fittings displayed. He put his heel solidly down on to the tangle of glass and metal, and mashed it into ruin. Then, extricating his foot with care, he went out with the rest.

Their journey, owing to the presence of the children, would have to be by fairly easy stages. John had planned for three days; the first march to take them to the end of Wensleydale, the second over the moors to a point north of Sedbergh, and the third, at last, to Blind Gill. It would be necessary to keep close to the main road, and he hoped that for long periods it would be possible to travel on it. He thought it was unlikely there would be any cars about. By now, Masham's example must have been followed in most of the North Riding. The cars would bog down long before they got to the Dale.

Roger said to him, as they made their way down by the side of a wood in the direction of Coverham:

'We could get hold of bicycles. What do you think?'

John shook his head. 'We would still be too vulnerable. And we should have to find ten bicycles together – otherwise it would mean having to wheel some along, or else splitting up the party.'

'And you're not going to do that, are you?' Roger asked.

John glanced at him. 'No. I'm not going to do that.'

Roger said: 'I'm glad Olivia was able to persuade the girl to come with us. It would have been grim to think of her back there.'

'You're getting sentimental, Rodge.'

'No.' Roger hitched his pack more firmly on to the middle of his back. 'You're toughening up. It's a good thing, I suppose.'

'Only suppose?'

'No. You're right, Johnny. It's got to be done. We're going to make it?'

'We're going to make it.'

The houses they passed were closed and shuttered; if people still lived in them they were giving no external sign of occupancy. They saw fewer people even than would have been normal in these parts; and when they did encounter others, there was no attempt at greeting on either side. For the most part, the people they met gave ground before the little party, and detoured round them. But twice they saw bands similar to their own. The first of these was of five adults, with two small children being carried. The two parties stared at each other briefly from a distance, and went their separate ways.

The second group was bigger than their own. There were

about a dozen people in it, all adults, and several guns were in evidence. This encounter happened in the afternoon, a few miles east of Aysgarth. Apparently this group was crossing the road on their way south to Bishopdale. They halted on the road, surveying the approach of John and the others.

John motioned his own group to a stop, about twenty yards away from them. There was a pause of observation. Then one of the men who faced them called:

'Where are ye from?'

John said: 'London.'

There was a ripple of hostile interest. Their leader said:

'There's little enough to be got in these parts for those who live here, without Londoners coming up scavenging.'

John made no reply. He hefted his shot-gun up under his arm, and Roger and Pirrie followed suit. They stared at the other group in silence.

'Where are ye making for?' the man asked them.

'We're going over the moors,' John said, 'into Westmorland.'

'There'll be nought more there than there is here.' His gaze was on the guns, longingly. 'If you can use those weapons, we might be willing to have you join up with us.'

'We can use them,' John said. 'But we prefer to stay on our own.'

'Safety in numbers these days.' John did not reply. 'Safer for the kiddies, and all.'

'We can look after them,' John said.

The man shrugged. He gestured to his followers, and they began to move off the road in their original direction. He himself prepared to follow them. At the road's edge, he paused, and turned back.

'Hey, mister!' he called. 'Any news?'

It was Roger who replied: 'None, but that the world's grown honest.'

The man's face cracked into a laugh. 'Ay, that's good. Then is doomsday near!'

They watched until the group was nearly out of sight, and then continued their journey.

They skirted to the south of Aysgarth, which showed signs

of defensive array that had now become familiar. They rested, in the afternoon's heat, within sight of the town. The valley, which had been so green in the old days, now showed predominantly black against the browner hills beyond. The stone walls wound their way up the hillsides, marking boundaries grown meaningless. Once John thought he saw sheep on the hillside, and jumped to his feet to make sure. But they were only white boulders. There could be no sheep here now. The Chung-Li virus had done its work with all-embracing thoroughness.

Mary was sitting with Olivia and the girl Jane. The boys, for once too tired to skylark, were resting together and discussing, so far as John could judge from the scraps of conversation he picked up, motor speedboats. Ann sat by herself, under a tree. He went over and sat down beside her.

'Are you feeling any better?' he asked her.

'I'm all right.'

She looked tired, and he wondered how much sleep she had managed to get the night before. He said:

'Only two more days of this, and then ... '

She caught his words up. 'And then everything's fine again, and we can forget all that's happened, and start life all over from the beginning. Well?'

'No. I don't suppose we can. Does it matter? But we can live what passes for a decent life again, and watch the children grow up into human beings instead of savages. That's worth doing a lot for.'

'And you're doing it, aren't you? The world on your shoulders.'

He said softly: 'We've been very lucky so far. It may not seem like that, but it's true. Lucky in getting away from London, and lucky in getting as far north as this before we ran into serious trouble. The reason this place looks deserted is because the locals have retired behind their defences, and the mobs haven't arrived. But I shouldn't think we're more than a day's march ahead of the mobs – we may be less. And when they come ... '

He stared at the tumbling waters of the Ure. It was a sunlit summer scene, strange only in the absence of so much of the familiar green. He didn't really believe the implications of his own words, and yet he knew they were true.

'We shall be at peace in Blind Gill,' Ann said wearily.

'I wouldn't mind being there now,' John said.

'I'm tired,' Ann said. 'I don't want to talk – about that or anything else. Let me be, John.'

He looked down at her for a moment, and then went away. As he did so, he saw that, from under the next tree, Millicent was watching them. She caught his eye, and smiled.

The valley narrowed towards Hawes, and the hills on either side rose more steeply; the stone walls no longer reached up to their summits. Hawes did not appear to be defended, but they avoided it all the same, going round on the higher ground to the south and fording the tributaries of the Ure, fortunately shallow at this time of year.

They made camp for the night in the mouth of Widdale Gill, securing themselves in the angle between the railway line and the river. Fairly near them they found a field that had been planted with potatoes, and dug up a good supply. Olivia made a stew of these and the salt meat they carried; Jane helped her and Millicent gave some half-hearted assistance.

The sun had set behind the Pennines, but it was still quite light; John looked at his watch and saw that it wasn't yet eight o'clock. Of course, that was British Summer Time, not Greenwich. He smiled at the thought of that delicate and ridiculous distinction.

They had done well, and the boys were not too obviously fatigued. Normally he might have taken them further before halting, but it would be stupid to begin the climb up into Mossdale in such circumstances. Instead, they could make an early start the following morning. He watched the preparations for supper with a contented eye. Pirrie was on guard beside the railway line.

The boys came over to him together. It was Davey who spoke; he used a tone of deference quite unlike his old man-to-man approach.

'Daddy,' he said, 'can we stand guard tonight as well?'

John surveyed them: the alert figure of his son, Spooks's gangling lankiness, Steve's rather square shortness. They were still just schoolboys, out on a more puzzling and exciting lark than usual.

He shook his head. 'Thanks very much for the offer, but we can manage.'

Davey said: 'But we've been working it out. It doesn't matter that we can't shoot properly as long as we can keep awake and make a noise if we see anyone. We can do that.'

John said: 'The best thing you three can do is not to stay awake talking after supper. Get to sleep as quickly as possible. We're up early in the morning, and we've got a stiff climb and a long day to face.'

He had spoken lightly enough, and in the old days Davey would have argued strenuously on the point. Now he only glanced at the other two boys in resignation, and they went off together to look at the river.

They all had supper together, Pirrie having come down from the line with a report of emptiness as far as the eye could see. Afterwards, John appointed the hours of sentry duty for the night.

Roger said: 'You're not counting Jane in?'

He thought Roger was joking at first, and laughed. Then he saw, to his astonishment, that it had been a serious question.

'No,' he said. 'Not tonight.'

The girl was sitting close to Olivia; she had not strayed far from her all day. John had heard them talking together during the afternoon, and had heard Jane laughing once. She glanced up at the two men, her fresh, somewhat fat-cheeked face open and inquiring.

'You wouldn't murder us in our beds, would you, Jane?' Roger asked her.

She shook her head solemnly.

John said to her: 'Well, it's best not to give you the chance, isn't it?'

She turned away, but it was in embarrassment, he saw, not hatred.

He said: 'It's Ann's first watch. The rest of us had better get down and get to sleep. You boys can put the fire out – tread out all the embers.'

Roger woke him, and handed him the shot-gun which the sentry kept. He got to his feet, feeling stiff, and rubbed his legs with his hands. The moon was up; its light gleamed on the nearby river, and threw shadows from the small group of huddled figures.

'Seasonably warm,' Roger said, 'thank God.'

'Anything to report?'

'What would there be, but ghosts?'

'Any ghosts, then?'

'A brief trace of one apparition – the corniest of them all.' John looked at him. 'The ghost train. I thought I heard it hooting in the distance, and for about ten minutes afterwards I could have sworn I heard its distant roar.'

'Could be a train,' John said. 'If there are any capable of being manned, and anyone capable of manning one, they might try a night journey. But I think it's a bit unlikely, taken all round.'

'I prefer to think of it as a ghost train. Heavily laden with the substantial ghosts of Dalesmen going to market, or trucks of ghostly coal or insubstantial metal ingots, crossing the Pennines. I've been thinking – how long do you think railway lines will be recognizable as railway lines? Twenty years – thirty? And how long will people remember that there were such things, once upon a time? Shall we tell fairy stories to our great-grandchildren about the metal monsters that ate coal and breathed out smoke?'

'Go to sleep,' John said. 'There'll be time enough to think about your great-grandchildren.'

'Ghosts,' Roger said. 'I see ghosts all round me tonight. The ghosts of my remote descendants, painted with woad.'

John made no reply, but climbed up the embankment to his post on the line. When he looked back from the top, Roger was curled up, and to all intents asleep.

The sentry's duty was to keep both sides of the line under observation, but the far side – the north – was more important owing to the fact that the main road lay in that direction. That was the sentry's actual post, out of direct sight of the group of sleepers. John took up his position there. He lit a cigarette, guarding the glowing end against possible observation. He didn't really think it was necessary, but it was natural to adapt old army tricks to a situation with so many familiar elements.

He looked at the small white cylinder, cupped in his hand. There was a habit that would have to go, but there was no point in ending it before necessity ended it for him. How long, he wondered, before the exploring Americans land at the forgotten harbours and push inland, handing out canned ham and cigars, and scattering Chung-Li immune grass seed on their way? In every little outpost, like Blind Gill, where the remnants of the British held out, something like that would be the common day-dream, the winter's tale. A legend, perhaps, that might spur the new barbarians at last across the western ocean, to find a land as rough and brutal as their own.

For he could no longer believe that there would be any last-minute reprieve for mankind. First China, and then the rest of Asia, and now Europe. The others would fall in their turn, incredulous, it might be, to the end. Nature was wiping a cloth across the slate of human history, leaving it empty for the pathetic scrawls of those few who, here and there over the face of the globe, would survive.

He heard a sound from the other side of the railway line, and moved warily across to investigate. As he reached the edge of the embankment, he saw that a slim figure was climbing the last few feet towards him. It was Millicent. She put a hand up to him and he grasped it.

He said: 'What the hell are you doing?'

She said: 'Ssh – you'll wake everyone up.'

She looked down at the sleeping group below, and then moved across towards the sentry post. John followed her. He was reasonably certain what the visit promised. The calm effrontery of it made him angry.

'You're not on duty for another couple of hours,' he said. 'You want to go back and get some sleep. We've got a long day in front of us.'

She asked him: 'Cigarette?' He took one from his case and gave it to her. 'Mind lighting it?'

He said: 'I don't think it's a good idea to show lights. Keep it under, and cover it with your hands when you inhale.'

'You know everything, don't you?'

She bent down to his cupped hands to take the lighter's flame. Her black hair gleamed in the moonlight. He was not, he realized, handling the situation very well. It had been a mistake to give her the cigarette she asked for; he should have sent her back to bed. She straightened up again, the cigarette now tucked behind her curled fingers.

'I can do without sleep,' she said. 'I remember one week-end I didn't have three hours sleep between Friday and Monday. Fresh as a daisy after it, too.'

'You don't have to boast. It's stamped all over you.'

'Is it?' There was a pause. 'What's the matter with Ann?'

He said coldly: 'You know as much as I do. I suppose it wouldn't have affected you – either what happened or what she did afterwards.'

Complacently, she said: 'There's one thing about not having very high standards – you're not likely to go off your rocker when you hit something nasty – either from other people or yourself.'

John drew on his cigarette. 'I don't want to talk about Ann. And I don't want an *affaire* with you – do you understand that? I should think you would see that, quite apart from anything else, this isn't the time for that sort of thing.'

'When you want a thing is the time to have it.'

'You've made a mistake. I don't want it.'

She laughed; her voice was lower when she did so, and rather hoarse.

'Let's be grown up,' she said. 'I may make mistakes, but not about that sort of thing.'

'You know my mind better than I do?'

'I shouldn't be surprised. I'll tell you this much, Big Chief. If it had been Olivia who had paid you this little visit, you would have sent her back straight away, and no back-answers. And why are you talking in whispers, anyway? In case we make anyone wake up?'

He had not realized that he had dropped his voice. He spoke more loudly: 'I think you'd better get back now, Millicent.'

She laughed again. 'What would be so unreasonable about not

wanting to wake people up? I don't suppose they're all as good at doing without sleep as I am. You rise too easily.'

'All right. I'm not going to argue with you. Just go back to bed, and forget all about it.'

She said obediently: 'O.K.' She dropped her cigarette, half smoked, and trod it into the ground. 'I'll just try the spark test, and if you don't fire, I'll go right down like a good little girl.'

She came towards him. He said: 'Don't be silly, Millicent.' She paused just short of him. 'Nothing wrong with a goodnight kiss, is there?' She put herself in his arms. He had to hold her or let her fall, and he held her. She was very warm, and softer to hold than he would have expected. She wriggled slightly against him.

'Spark test satisfactory, I think,' she said.

They both turned at the sound of small stones falling. A figure rose above the embankment's edge and stood facing them.

Pirrie tapped his rifle, which he held under his arm. He said reprovingly: 'Even carrying this, I very nearly surprised you. You are not as alert as a good sentry should be, Custance.'

Millicent had disengaged herself. She said: 'What do you think you're doing, wandering around in the middle of the night?'

'Would it be altogether inappropriate,' Pirrie asked, 'to put a similar question to you?'

She said scornfully: 'I thought the eyeful you got the last time you spied on me had put you off. Or is that the way you get your kick now?'

Pirrie said: 'The last several times, I have borne with the situation as the lesser evil. I will grant that you have been discreet. Any action I might have taken could only have made my cuckoldry conspicuous, and I was always anxious to avoid that.'

'Don't worry,' Millicent said. 'I'll go on being discreet.'

John said: 'Pirrie! Nothing has happened between your wife and me. Nothing is going to. The only thing I am concerned with is getting us all safely to Blind Gill.'

In a musing tone, Pirrie said: 'My natural inclination always was to kill her. But in normal society, murder is much too great a risk. I went so far as to make plans, and rather good ones, too, but I would never have carried them out.'

Millicent said: 'Henry! Don't start being silly.'

In the moonlight, John saw Pirrie lift his right hand, and rub the fingers along the side of his nose. He said sharply:

'That's enough of that!'

Deliberately, Pirrie released the safety catch on the rifle. John raised his shot-gun.

'No,' Pirrie said calmly. 'Put that gun down. You are very well aware that I could shoot a good deal more quickly than you. Put it down. I should not care to be provoked into a rash act.'

John lowered the shot-gun. In any case it had been ridiculous, he thought, to envisage Pirrie as a figure out of an Elizabethan tragedy.

He said: 'Things must be getting me down. It was a silly thought, wasn't it? If you'd really wanted to dish Millicent, there was nothing to stop you leaving her in London.'

'A good point,' Pirrie said, 'but invalid. You must remember that although I joined your party I did so with reservations as to the truth of the story Buckley asked me to believe. I was willing to engage with you in breaking out of the police cordon because I am extremely devoted to my liberty of action. That was all.'

Millicent said: 'You two can continue the chat. I'm going back to bed.'

'No,' Pirrie said softly, 'stay where you are. Stay exactly where you are.' He touched the barrel of his rifle, and she halted the movement she had just begun. 'I may say that I gave serious, if brief, consideration to the idea of leaving Millicent behind in London. One reason for rejecting it was my assurance that, if nothing worse occurred than civil break-down, Millicent would manage very well by dint of offering her erotic services to the local gang-leader. I did not care for the idea of abandoning her to what might prove an extremely successful career.'

'Would it have mattered?' John asked.

'I am not,' said Pirrie, 'a person on whom humiliation sits lightly. There is a strain in my make-up that some might describe as primitive. Tell me, Custance – we are agreed that the process of law no longer exists in this country?'

'If it does, we'll all hang.'

'Exactly. Now, if State law fails, what remains?'

John said carefully: 'The law of the group – for its own protection.'

'And of the family?'

'Within the group. The needs of the group come first.'

'And the head of the family?' Millicent began to laugh, a nervous almost hysterical laugh. 'Amuse yourself, my dear,' Pirrie continued. 'I like to see you happy. Well, Custance. The man is the proper head of his family group – are we still agreed?'

There was only one direction in which the insane relentless logic could be heading. John said:

'Yes. Within the group.' He hesitated. 'I am in charge here. The final say is mine.'

He thought Pirrie smiled, but in the dim light it was difficult to be sure. Pirrie said:

'The final say is here.' He tapped the rifle. 'I can, if I wish, destroy the group. I am a wronged husband, Custance – a jealous one, perhaps, or a proud one. I am determined to have my rights. I hope you will not gainsay me, for I should not like to have to oppose you.'

'You know the way to Blind Gill now,' John said. 'But you might have difficulty getting entry without me.'

'I have a good weapon, and I can use it. I believe I should find employment quite readily.'

There was a pause. In the silence there came a sudden bubbling lift of bird song; with a shock John recognized it as a nightingale.

'Well,' Pirrie said, 'do you concede me my rights?'

Millicent cried: 'No! John, stop him. He can't behave like this – it isn't human. Henry, I promise . . . '

'To cease upon the midnight,' Pirrie said, 'with no pain. Even I can recognize the appositeness of verse occasionally. Custance! Do I have my rights?'

Moonlight silvered the barrel as it swung to cover John again. Suddenly he was afraid – not only for himself, but for Ann and the children also. There was no doubt about Pirrie's implacability; the only doubt was as to where, with provocation, it might lead him.

'Take your rights,' he said.

In a voice shocked and unfamiliar, Millicent said: 'No! Not here . . .'

She ran towards Pirrie, stumbling awkwardly over the railway lines. He waited until she was almost on him before he fired. Her body spun backwards with the force of the bullet, and lay across one of the lines. From the hills, the echoes of the shot cracked back.

John walked across the lines, passing close by the body. Pirrie had put down his rifle. John stood beside him and looked down the embankment. They had all awakened with the sound of the shot.

He called down: 'It's all right. Everybody go to sleep again. Nothing to worry about.'

Roger shouted up: 'That wasn't the shot-gun. Is Pirrie up there?'

'Yes,' John said. 'You can turn in. Everything's under control.'

Pirrie turned and looked at him. 'I think I will turn in, too.'

John said sharply: 'You can give me a hand with this first. We can't leave it here for the women to brood over while they're on watch.'

Pirrie nodded. 'The river?'

'Too shallow. It would probably stick. And I don't think it's a good idea to pollute water supplies anyway. Down the embankment, on the other side of the river. I should think that will do.'

They carried the body along the line to a point about two hundred yards west. It was light, but the going was difficult. John was relieved when the time came to throw it down the embankment. There were bushes at the foot; it landed among them. It was possible to see Millicent's white blouse but, in the moonlight, nothing more.

John and Pirrie walked back together in silence. When they reached the sentry point, John said:

'You can go down now. But I shall tell Olivia to wake you for what would have been your wife's shift. No objections, I take it?'

Pirrie said mildly: 'Of course. Whatever you say.' He tucked his rifle under his arm. 'Good night, Custance.'

'Good night,' John said.

He watched Pirrie slithering his way down the slope towards the others. He could have been mistaken, of course. It might have been possible to save Millicent's life.

He was surprised to find that the thought did not worry him.

NINE

In the morning, a subdued air was evident. John had told them that Pirrie had shot Millicent, but had let the children think it was an accident. He gave a full account to Roger, who shook his head.

'Cool, isn't he? We certainly picked up something when we adopted him.'

'Yes,' John said, 'we did.'

'Are you going to have trouble, do you think?'

'Not as long as I let him have his own way,' John said. 'Fortunately, his needs seem fairly modest. He felt he had a right to kill his own wife.'

Ann came down to him later, when he was washing in the river. She stood beside him, and looked at the tumbling waters. The sun was shining the length of the valley, but there were clouds directly above them, large and close-pressed.

'Where did you put the body?' she asked him. 'Before I send the children down to wash.'

'Well away from here. You can send them down.'

She looked at him without expression. 'You might as well tell me what happened. Pirrie isn't the sort to have accidents with a rifle, or to kill without a reason.'

He told her, making no attempt to hide anything.

She said: 'And if Pirrie had not appeared just at that moment?'

He shrugged. 'I would have sent her back down, I think. What else can I say?'

'Nothing, I suppose. It doesn't matter now.' She shot the question at him suddenly: 'Why didn't you save her?'

'I couldn't. Pirrie had made up his mind. I would only have got myself shot as well.'

She said bitterly: 'You're the leader. Are you going to stand by and let people murder each other?'

He looked at her. His voice was cold. 'I thought my life was worth more to you and the children than Millicent's. I still think so, whether you agree or not.'

For the moment they faced each other in silence; then Ann came a step towards him, and he caught her. He heard her whisper:

'Darling, I'm sorry. You know I didn't mean that. But it's so terrible, and it goes on getting worse. To kill his wife like that. . . . What kind of a life is it going to be for us?'

'When we get to Blind Gill . . .'

'We shall still have Pirrie with us, shan't we? Oh, John, must we? Can't we – lose him somehow?'

He said gently: 'You're worrying too much. Pirrie is law-abiding enough. I think he had hated Millicent for years. There's been a lot of bloodshed recently, and I suppose it went to his head. It will be different in the valley. We shall have our own law and order. Pirrie will conform.'

'Will he?'

He stroked her arms. 'You,' he said. 'How is it now? Not quite so bad?'

She shook her head. 'Not quite so bad. I suppose one gets used to everything, even memories.'

By seven o'clock they were all together, and ready to set out. The clouds which had come over the sky still showed gaps of blue, but they had spread far enough to the east to hide the sun.

'Weather less promising,' Roger said.

'We don't want it too hot,' John said. 'We have a climb in front of us. Everything ready?'

Pirrie said: 'I should like Jane to walk with me.'

They stared at him. The request was so odd as to be meaningless in itself. John had not thought it necessary to have the party walk in any particular order, with the result that they straggled along in whatever way they chose. Jane had automatically taken up her position alongside Olivia again.

John said: 'Why?'

Pirrie gazed round the little circle with untroubled eyes. 'Perhaps I should put it another way. I have decided that I should like to marry Jane – insofar as the expression has any meaning now.'

Olivia said, with a sharpness quite out of keeping with her

usual manner: 'Don't be ridiculous. There can't be any question of that.'

Pirrie said mildly: 'I see no bar. Jane is an unmarried girl, and I am a widower.'

Jane, John saw, was looking at Pirrie with wide and intent eyes; it was impossible to read her expression.

Ann said: 'Mr Pirrie, you killed Millicent last night. Isn't that enough bar?'

The boys were watching the scene in fascination; Mary turned her head away. It had been silly, John thought wearily, to imagine this world was a world in which any kind of innocence could be preserved.

'No,' Pirrie said, 'I don't regard it as a bar.'

Roger said: 'You also killed Jane's father.'

Pirie nodded. 'An unfortunate necessity. I'm sure Jane has resigned herself to that.'

John said: 'I suggest we leave things over for now, Pirrie. Jane knows your mind. She can think about it for the next day or two.

'No.' Pirrie put out his hand. 'Come here, Jane.'

Jane stood, still gazing at him. Olivia said:

'Leave her alone. You're not to touch her. You've done enough, without adding this.'

Pirrie ignored her. He repeated: 'Come here, Jane. I am not a young man, nor a particularly handsome one. But I can look after you, which is more than many young men could do in the present circumstances.'

Ann said: 'Look after her – or murder her?'

'Millicent,' Pirrie said, 'had been unfaithful to me a number of times, and was attempting to be so again. That is the only reason for her being dead.'

Incredulously, Ann said: 'You speak as though women were another kind of creature – less than human.'

Pirrie said courteously: 'I'm sorry if you think so. Jane! Come with me.'

They watched in silence as, slowly, Jane went over to where Pirrie waited for her. Pirrie took her hands in his. He said: 'I think we shall get on very well together.'

Olivia said: 'No, Jane – you mustn't!'

'And now,' said Pirrie, 'I think we can move off.'

'Roger, John,' Olivia said. 'Stop him!'

Roger looked at John. John said: 'I don't think it's anything to do with the rest of us.'

'What if it had been Mary?' Olivia said. 'Jane has rights as much as any of us.'

'You're wasting your time, Olivia,' John said. 'It's a different world we're living in. The girl went over to Pirrie of her own free will. There's nothing else to be said. Off we go now.'

Ann walked beside him as they set off, walking along the railway line. The valley narrowed sharply ahead of them, and the road, to the north, veered in towards them.

'There's something horrible about Pirrie,' Ann said. 'A coldness and a brutality. It's terrible to think of putting that young girl in his hands.'

'She did go to him voluntarily.'

'Because she was afraid! The man's a killer.'

'We all are.'

'Not in the same way. You didn't make any attempt to stop it, did you? You and Roger could have stopped him. It wasn't like the business with Millicent. You were only a couple of feet from him.'

'And he had the safety catch on. Either of us could have shot him.'

'Well?'

'If there had been ten Janes and he had wanted them all, he could have had them. Pirrie's worth more to us than they would be.'

'And if it had been Mary – as Olivia said?'

'Pirrie would have shot me before he mentioned the matter. He could have done so last night, you know, and very easily. I may be the leader here, but we're still kept together by mutual consent. It doesn't matter whether that consent is inspired by fear or not, as long as it holds. Pirrie and I are not going to frighten each other; we each know the other's necessary. If either of us were put out of action, it might mean the difference between getting to the valley or not.'

She said intensely: 'And when we get there – will you be prepared to deal with Pirrie then?'

'Wait till we get there. As to that –'

He smiled, and she noticed it. 'What?'

'I don't think Jane's the kind of girl to remain afraid for long. She will shake herself out of it. And when she does ... I wouldn't trust her on night watch – Pirrie proposes taking her to bed with him. It seems odd to think of Pirrie as being over trustful – all the same, he's already been mistaken in one wife.'

'Even if she wanted to,' Ann said, 'what could she do? He may not look much, but he's strong.'

'That's up to you and Olivia, isn't it? You keep the cutlery items.'

She looked at him, trying to estimate how seriously the remark had been intended.

'But not until we get to the valley,' he said. 'She will have to put up with him until then, at any rate.'

As they climbed up to Mossdale Head, the sky darkened continually, and gusts of rain swept in their faces. These increased as they neared the ridge, and they breasted it to see the western sky black and stormy over the rolling moors. They had four light plastic mackintoshes in the packs, which John told the women to put on. The boys would have to learn to contend with being wet; although the temperature was lower than it had been, the day was still reasonably warm.

The rain thickened as they walked on. Within half an hour, men and boys were both soaked. John had crossed the Pennines by this route before, but only by car. There had been a sense of isolation about the pass even then, a feeling of being in a country swept of life, despite the road and the railway line that hugged it.

That feeling now was more than doubly intensified. There were few things, John thought, so desolate as a railway line on which no train could be expected. And where the pattern of the moors seen from a moving car had been monotonous, the monotony to people on foot, struggling through rain squalls, was far greater. The moors themselves were barer, of course. The heather still grew, but the moorland grasses were gone; the outcrops of rocks jutted like teeth in the head of a skull.

During the morning, they passed occasional small parties heading in the opposite direction. Once again, there was mutual suspicion and avoidance. One group of three had their belongings strapped on a donkey. John and the others stared at it with amazement. Someone presumably had kept it alive on dry fodder after the other beasts of burden were killed along with the cattle, but once away from its barn it would have to starve.

Roger said: 'A variation of the old sleigh-dog technique, I imagine. You get it to take you as far as you can, and then eat it.'

'It's a standing temptation to any other party you happen to meet, though, isn't it?' John said. 'I can't see them getting very far with that once they reach the Dale.'

Pirrie said: 'We could relieve them of it now.'

'No,' John said. 'It isn't worth our while, in any case. We've got enough meat to last us, and we should reach Blind Gill tomorrow. It would only be unnecessary weight.'

Steve began limping shortly afterwards, and examination showed him to have a blistered heel.

Olivia said: 'Steve! Why didn't you say something when it first started hurting?'

He looked at the adult faces surrounding him, and his ten-year-old assurance deserted him. He began to cry.

'There's nothing to cry about, old man,' Roger said. 'A blistered heel is bad luck, but it's not the end of the world.'

His sobs were not the ordinary sobs of childhood, but those in which experience beyond a child's range was released from its confinement. He said something, and Roger bent down to catch his words.

'What was that, Steve?'

'If I couldn't walk – I thought you might leave me.'

Roger and Olivia looked at each other. Roger said:

'Nobody's going to leave you. How on earth could you think that?'

'Mr Pirrie left Millicent,' Steve said.

John intervened. 'He'd better not walk on it. It will only get worse.'

'I'll carry him,' Roger said. 'Spooks, will you carry my gun for me?'

Spooks nodded. 'I'd like to.'

'You and I will take him in turns, Rodge,' John said. 'We'll manage him all right. Good job he's a little 'un.'

Olivia said: 'Roger and I can take the turns. He's our boy. We can carry him.'

She had not spoken to John since the incident of Jane and Pirrie. John said to her:

'Olivia – I do the arranging around here. Roger and I will carry Steve. You can take the pack of whoever happens to be doing it at the time.'

Their eyes held for a moment, and then she turned away.

Roger said: 'All right, old son. Up you get.'

Their progress immediately after this was a little faster, since Steve had been acting as a brake, but John was not deceived by it. The carrying of a passenger, even a boy as small as Steve, added to their difficulties. He kept them going until they had nearly got to the end of Garsdale, before he called a halt to their midday meal.

The wind, which had been carrying the rain into their faces, had dropped, but the rain itself was still falling, and in a steadier and more soaking downpour. John looked round the unpromising scene.

'Anybody see a cave and a pile of firewood stacked inside? I thought not. A cold snack today, and water. And we can rest our legs a little.'

Ann said: 'Couldn't we find somewhere dry to eat it?'

About fifty yards along the road, there was a small house, standing back. John followed her gaze towards it.

'It might be empty,' he said. 'But we should have to go up to it and find out, shouldn't we? And then it might not be empty after all. I don't mind us taking risks when it's for something we must have, like food, but isn't worth it for half an hour's shelter.'

'Davey's soaked,' she said.

'Half an hour won't dry him out. And that's all the time we can spare.' He called to the boy: 'How are you, Davey? Wet?'

Davey nodded. 'Yes, Dad.'

'Try laughing drily.'

It was an old joke. Davey did his best to smile at it. John went over and rumpled his wet hair.

'You're doing fine,' he said. 'Really fine.'

The western approach to Garsdale had been through a narrow strip of good grazing land which now, in the steady rain, was a band of mud, studded here and there with farm buildings. They looked down to Sedbergh, resting between hills and valley on the other side of the Rawthey. Smoke lay above it, and drifted westwards along the edge of the moors. Sedburgh was burning.

'Looters,' Roger said.

John swung his glasses over the stone-built town.

'We're meeting the north-western stream now; and they've had the extra day to get here. All the same, it's a bit of a shaker. I thought this part would still be quiet.'

'It might not be so bad,' Roger said, 'if we cut north straight away and get past on the higher ground. It might not be so bad up in the Lune valley.'

Pirrie said: 'When a town like that goes under, I should expect all the valleys around to be in a dangerous condition. It is not going to be easy.'

John had directed the glasses beyond the ravaged town to the mouth of the dale along which they had proposed to travel. He could make out movements but it was impossible to know what they constituted. Smoke rose from isolated buildings. There was an alternative route, across the moors to Kendal, but that also took them over the Lune. In any case if Sedburgh had fallen was there any reason to think things were any better around Kendal?

Pirrie glanced at him speculatively. 'If I may offer a comment, I think we are under-armed for the conditions that lie ahead. Those people with the donkey – we should probably have got a gun or two out of them, apart from the animal. They would hardly have had the temerity to travel as they were doing, unarmed.'

Roger said: 'It might not be as bad as it looks. We shall have to make the effort, anyway.'

John looked out over the confluence of valleys and rivers.

'I don't know. We may find ourselves walking into something we can't cope with. It might be too late then.'

'We can't stay here, can we?' said Roger. 'And we can't go back, so we must go forward.'

John turned towards Pirrie. He realized, as he did so, that, although Roger might be his friend, Pirrie was his lieutenant. It was Pirrie's coolness and judgement on which he had come to rely.

'I think we need more than just guns. There aren't enough of us. If we're going to be sure of getting to Blind Gill, we shall have to snowball. What do you think?'

Pirrie nodded, considering the point. 'I'm inclined to agree. Three men are no longer an adequate number for defence.'

Roger said impatiently: 'What do we do then? Hang out a banner, with a sign on it: "Recruits Welcomed"?'

'I suggest we make a halt here,' John said. 'We're still on the pass, and we'll get parties going both ways across the Pennines. They will be less likely to be downright looters, too. The looters will be happy enough down in the valleys.'

They looked again down the vista their position commanded. Even in the rain it was very picturesque. And, even in the rain, the houses down there were burning.

Pirrie said thoughtfully: 'We could ambush parties as they came through – there's enough cover about a hundred yards back.'

'There aren't enough of us to make a press-gang,' John said. 'We need volunteers. After all, if they have guns we should have to give them back to them.'

Roger said: 'What do we do, then? Make camp? By the side of the road?'

'Yes,' John said. He looked at his bedraggled group of followers. 'Let's hope not for long.'

They had to wait over an hour for their first encounter, and then it was a disappointing one. They saw a little party struggling up the road from the valley, and, as they drew nearer, could see that they were eight in number. There were four women, two children – a boy about eight and a girl who looked younger – and two men. They were wheeling two perambulators, stacked high with household goods; a saucepan fell off when they were about fifty yards away and rolled away with a clatter. One of the women stooped down wearily to pick it up.

The two men, like their womenfolk, looked miserable and scared. One of them was well over fifty; the other, although quite young, was physically weedy.

Pirrie said: 'I hardly think there is anything here that will be to our advantage.'

He and Roger were standing with John on the road itself, holding their guns. The women and children were resting on a flat-topped stone wall nearby.

John shook his head. 'I think you're right. No weapons, either, I should think. One of the kids may have a water-pistol.'

The approaching party stopped when they caught sight of the three men standing in the road, but after a whispered consultation and a glance backwards into the smouldering valley, they came on again. Fear stood on them more markedly now. The older man walked in front, and tried to look unconcerned, with poor success. The girl began to cry, and one of the women tugged at her, simultaneously frantic and furtive, as though afraid the noise would in some way betray them.

As they passed, in silence, John thought how natural it would have been, a few days before, to give some kind of greeting, and how unnatural the same greeting would have sounded now.

Roger said quietly: 'How far do you think they'll get?'

'Down into Wensleydale, possibly. I don't know. They may survive a week, if they're lucky.'

'Lucky? Or unlucky?'

'Yes. Unlucky, I suppose.'

Pirrie said: 'They appear to be turning back.'

John looked. They had travelled perhaps seventy-five yards farther on along the road; now they had turned and were making their way back, still pushing the perambulators. By turning, they had got the rain in their faces instead of on their backs. The little girl's mackintosh gaped at the neck; her fingers fumbled, trying to fasten it, but she could not.

They stopped a short distance away. The older man said:

'We wondered if you was waiting for anything up here – if there was anything we could tell you, maybe.'

John's eyes examined him. A manual worker of some kind; the sort of man who would give a lifetime's faithful inefficient service. On his own, under the new conditions, he would have small chance of survival, his only hope lying in the possibility of attaching himself to some little Napoleonic gangster of the dales who would put up with his uselessness for the sake of his devotion. With his present entourage, even that was ruled out.

'No,' John said. 'There's nothing you can tell us.'

'We was heading across the Pennines,' the man went on. 'We reckoned it might be quieter over in those parts. We thought we might find a farm or something, out of the way, where they'd let us work and give us some food. We wouldn't want much.'

A few months ago, the pipe-dream had probably been a £75,000 win on the football pools. Their chances of that had been about as good as the chances of their more modest hopes were now. He looked at the four women; only one of them was sufficiently youthful to stand a chance of surviving on sexual merits, and with youth her entire store of assets were numbered. They were all bedraggled. The two children had wandered away, in the direction of the wall where Ann and the others were sitting. The boy was not wearing shoes, but plimsolls, which were wet through.

John said harshly: 'You'd better get on, then, hadn't you?'

The man persisted: 'You think we might find a place like that?'

'You might,' John said.

'All this trouble,' one of the women said. 'It won't last long, will it?'

Roger looked down into the valley. 'Only till hell freezes over.'

'Where was you thinking of heading?' asked the older man. 'Were you thinking of going into Yorkshire as well?'

John said: 'No. We've come from there.'

'We're not bothered about which way we go, for that matter. We only thought it might be quieter across the Pennines.'

'Yes. It might.'

The mother of the two children spoke: 'What my father means is – do you think we could go whichever way you're going? It would mean there was more of us, if we ran into any trouble. I mean – you must be looking for a quiet place, too. You're respectable people, not like those down there. Respectable folk should stick together at a time like this.'

John said: 'There are something like fifty million people in this country. Probably over forty-nine million of them are respectable, and looking for a quiet place. There aren't enough quiet places to go round.'

'Yes, that's why it's better for folks to stick together. Respectable folk.'

'How long have you been on the road?' John asked her.

She looked puzzled. 'We started this morning – we could see fires in Sedburgh, and they were burning the Follins farm, and that's not more than three miles from the village.'

'We've had three days' start on you. We aren't respectable any longer. We've killed people on our way here, and we may have to kill more. I think you'd better carry on by yourselves, as you were doing.'

They stared at him. The older man said at last:

'I suppose you had to. I suppose a man's got to save himself and his family any way he can. They got me on killing in the First War, and the Jerries hadn't burned Sedburgh then, nor the Follins farm. If you've got to do things, then you've got to.'

John did not reply. At the wall, the two children were playing with the others, scrambling up and along the wall and down in a complicated kind of obstacle race. Ann saw his glance, and rose to come towards him.

'Can we go with you?' the man said. 'We'll do as you say – I don't mind killing if it's necessary, and we can do our share of the work. We don't mind which way you're going – it's all the same as far as we're concerned. Apart from being in the army, I've lived all my life in Carbeck. Now I've had to leave it, it doesn't matter where I go.'

'How many guns have you got?' John asked.

He shook his head. 'We haven't got any guns.'

'We've got three, to look after six adults and four children. Even that isn't enough. That's why we're waiting here – to find others who've got guns and who will join up with us. I'm sorry, but we can't take passengers.'

'We wouldn't be passengers! I can turn my hand to most

things. I can shoot, if you can come by another gun. I was a sharpshooter in the Fusiliers.'

'If you were by yourself, we might have you. As it is, with four women and two more children . . . we can't afford to take on extra handicaps.'

The rain had stopped, but the sky remained grey and formless, and it was rather cold. The younger man, who had still not spoken, shivered and pulled his dirty raincoat more tightly round him.

The other man said desperately: 'We've got food. In the pram – half a side of bacon.'

'We have enough. We killed to get it, and we can kill again.'

The mother said: 'Don't turn us down. Think of the children. You wouldn't turn us down with the children.'

'I'm thinking of my own children,' John said. 'If I were able to think of any others, there would be millions I could think of. If I were you, I should get moving. If you're going to find your quiet place, you want to find it before the mob does.'

They looked at him, understanding what he said but unwilling to believe that he could be refusing them.

Ann said, close beside him: 'We could take them, couldn't we? The children . . . ' He looked at her. 'Yes – I haven't forgotten what I said – about Spooks. I was wrong.'

'No,' John said. 'You were right. There's no place for pity now.'

With horror, she said: 'Don't say that.'

He gestured towards the smoke, rising in the valley. 'Pity always was a luxury. It's all right if the tragedy's a comfortable distance away – if you can watch it from a seat in the cinema. It's different when you find it on your doorstep – on every doorstep.'

Olivia had also come over from the wall. Jane, who had made little response to Olivia, following her morning of walking with Pirrie, also left the wall, but went and stood near Pirrie. He glanced at her, but said nothing.

Olivia said: 'I can't see that it would hurt to let them tag along. And they might be some help.'

'They let the boy come on the road in plimsolls,' John said, 'in this weather. You should have understood by now, Olivia, that it's not only the weakest but the least efficient as well who are going to go to the wall. They couldn't help us; they could hinder.'

The boy's mother said: 'I told him to put his boots on. We didn't see that he hadn't until we were a couple of miles from the village. And then we daren't go back.'

John said wearily: 'I know. I'm simply saying that there's no scope for forgetting to notice things any more. If you didn't notice the boy's feet, you might not notice something more important. And every one of us might die as a result. I don't feel like taking the chance. I don't feel like taking any chances.'

Olivia said: 'Roger . . . '

Roger shook his head. 'Things have changed in the last three days. When Johnny and I tossed that coin for leadership, I didn't take it seriously. But he's the boss now, isn't he? He's willing to take it all on his conscience, and that lets the rest of us out. He's probably right, anyway.'

The newcomers had been following the interchange with fascination. Now the older man, seeing in Roger's acquiescence the failure of their hopes, turned away, shaking his head. The mother of the children was not so easily shaken off.

'We can follow you,' she said. 'We can stay here till you move and then follow you. You can't stop us doing that.'

John said: 'You'd better go now. It won't do any good talking.'

'No, we'll stay! You can't make us go.'

Pirrie intervened, for the first time: 'We cannot make you go; but we can make you stay here after we've gone.' He touched his rifle. 'I think you would be wiser to go now.'

The woman said, but lacking conviction: 'You wouldn't do it.'

Ann said bitterly: 'He would. We depend on him. You'd better go.'

The woman looked into both their faces; then she turned and called to her children: 'Bessie! Wilf!'

They detached themselves from the others with reluctance. It was like any occasion on which children meet and then, at the whim of their parents, must break away again, their friendship only tentatively begun. Ann watched them come.

She said to John: 'Please . . . '

He shook his head. 'I have to do what's best for us. There are millions of others – these are only the ones we see.'

'Charity is for those we see.'

'I told you – charity, pity . . . they come from a steady income and money to spare. We're all bankrupt now.'

Pirrie said: 'Custance! Up the road, there.'

Between Baugh Fell and Rise Hill, the road ran straight for about three-quarters of a mile. There were figures on it, coming down towards them.

This was a large party – seven or eight men, with women and some children. They walked with confidence along the crown of the road, and even at that distance they were accompanied by what looked like the glint of guns.

John said with satisfaction: 'That's what we want.'

Roger said: 'If they'll talk. They may be the kind that shoot first. We could get over behind the wall before we try opening the conversation.'

'If we did, it might give them reason to shoot first.'

'The women and children, then.'

'Same thing. Their own are out in the open.'

The older man of the other party said: 'Can we stay with you till these have gone past, then?'

John was on the verge of refusing when Pirrie caught his eye. He nodded his head very slightly. John caught the point: a temporary augmentation, if only in numbers and not in strength, might be a bargaining point.

He said indifferently: 'If you like.'

They watched the new group approach. After a time the children, Bessie and Wilf, drifted away and back to where the others were still playing on the wall.

Most of the men seemed to be carrying guns. John could eventually make out a couple of army pattern .300 rifles, a Winchester .202, and the inevitable shot-guns. With increasing assurance, he thought: this is it. This was enough to get them through any kind of chaos to Blind Gill. There only remained the problem of winning them over.

He had hoped they would halt a short distance away, but they had neither suspicion nor doubts of their own ability to meet any challenge, and they came on. Their leader was a burly man, with a heavy red face. He wore a leather belt, with a revolver stuck in it. As he came abreast of where John's party stood by the side of the road, he glanced at them indifferently. It was another good sign that he did not covet their guns; or not enough, at least, even to contemplate fighting for them.

John called to him: 'Just a minute.'

He stopped and looked at John with a deliberation of movement that was impressive. His accent, when he spoke was thickly Yorkshire.

'You wanted summat?'

'My name's John Custance. We're heading for a place I know, up in the hills. My brother's got land there – in a valley that's blocked at one end and only a few feet wide at the other. Once in there, you can keep an army out. Are you interested?'

He considered for a moment. 'What are you telling us for?'

John pointed down towards the valley. 'Things are nasty down there. Too nasty for a small party like ours. We're looking for recruits.'

The man grinned. 'Happen we're not looking for a change. We're doin' all right.'

'You're doing all right now,' John said, 'while there are potatoes in the ground, and meat to be looted from farmhouses. But it won't be too long before the meat's used up, and there won't be any to follow it. You won't find potatoes in the fields next year, either.'

'We'll look after that when the time comes.'

'I can tell you how. By cannibalism. Are you looking forward to it?'

The leader himself was still contemptuously hostile, but there was some response, John thought, in the ranks behind him. He could not have had long to weld his band together; there would be cross-currents, perhaps counter-currents.

The man said: 'Maybe we'll have the taste for it by then. I don't think as I could fancy you at the moment.'

'It's up to you,' John said. He looked past him to where the women and children were; there were five women, and four children, their ages varying between five and fifteen. 'Those who can't find a piece of land which they can hold are going to end up by being savages – if they survive at all. That may suit you. It doesn't suit us.'

'I'll tell you what doesn't suit me, mister – a lot of talk. I never had no time for gabbers.'

'You won't need to talk at all in a few years,' John said. 'You'll be back to grunts and sign language. I'm talking because I've got something to tell you, and if you've got any sense you will see it's to your advantage to listen.'

'Our advantage, eh? It wouldn't be yours you're thinking about?'

'I'd be a fool if it wasn't. But you stand to get more out of it. We want temporary help so that we can get to my brother's place. We're offering you a place where you can live in something like peace, and rear your children to be something better than wild animals.'

The man glanced round at his followers, as though sensing an effect that John's words were having on them. He said:

'Still talk. You think we're going to take you on, and find ourselves on a wild-goose chase up in the hills?'

'Have you got a better place to go to? Have you got anywhere to go to, for that matter? What harm can it possibly do you to come along with us and find out?'

He stared at John, still hostile but baffled. At last, he turned to his followers.

'What do you reckon of it?' he said to them.

Before anyone spoke, he must have read the answer in their expressions.

'Wouldn't do any harm to go and have a look,' a dark, thick-set man said. There was a murmur of agreement. The red-faced man turned back to John.

'Right,' he said. 'You can show us the way to this valley of your brother's. We'll see what we think of it when we get there. Where abouts is it, anyway?'

Unprepared to reveal the location of Blind Gill, or even to name it, John was getting ready an evasive answer, when Pirrie intervened. He said coolly:

'That's Mr Custance's business, not yours. He's in charge here. Do as he tells you, and you will be all right.'

John heard a gasp of dismay from Ann. He himself found it hard to see a justification for Pirrie's insolence, both of manner and content; it could only re-confirm the leader of the other group in his hostility. He thought of saying something to take the edge off the remark, but was stopped both by the realization that he wouldn't be likely to mend the situation, and by the trust he had come to have in Pirrie's judgement. Pirrie, undoubtedly, knew what he was doing.

'It's like that, is it?' the man said. 'We're to do as Custance tells us? You can think again about that. I do the ordering for my lot, and, if you join up with us, the same goes for you.'

'You're a big man,' Pirrie observed speculatively, 'but what the situation needs is brains. And there, I imagine, you fall short.'

The red-faced man spoke with incongruous softness:

'I don't take anything from little bastards just because they're little. There aren't any policemen round the corner now. I make my own regulations; and one of them is that people round me keep their tongues civil.'

Finishing, he tapped the revolver in his belt, to emphasize his words. As he did so, Pirrie raised his rifle. The man, in earnest now, began to pull the revolver out. But the muzzle was still inside his belt when Pirrie fired. From that short range, the bullet lifted him and crashed him backwards on the road. Pirrie stood in silence, his rifle at the ready.

Some of the women screamed. John's eyes were on the men opposing him. He had restrained his impulse to raise his own shot-gun, and was glad to see that Roger also had not moved. Some of the other men made tentative movements towards their guns, but the incident had occurred too quickly for them, and too surprisingly. One of them half lifted a rifle; unconcernedly, Pirrie moved to cover him, and he set it down again.

John said: 'It's a pity about that.' He glanced at Pirrie. 'But he should have known better than to try threatening someone with a gun if he wasn't sure he could fire first. Well, the offer's still open. Anyone who wants to join us and head for the valley is welcome.'

One of the women had knelt down by the side of the fallen man. She looked up.

'He's dead.'

John nodded slightly. He looked at the others.

'Have you made up your minds yet?'

The thick-set man, who had spoken before, said:

'I reckon it were his own look-out. I'll come along, all right. My name's Parsons – Alf Parsons.'

Slowly, with an air almost ritualistic, Pirrie lowered his rifle. He went across to the body, and pulled the revolver out of the belt. He took it by the muzzle, and handed it to John. Then he turned back to address the others:

'My name is Pirrie, and this is Buckley, on my right. As I said, Mr Custance is in charge here. Those who wish to join up with our little party should come along and shake hands with Mr Custance, and identify themselves. All right?'

Alf Parsons was the first to comply, but the others lined up behind him. Here, more than ever, ritual was being laid down. It might come, in time, to a bending of the knee, but this formal hand-shake was as clear a sign as that would have been of the rendering of fealty.

For himself, John saw, it signified a new role, of enhanced power. The leadership of his own small party, accidental at first, into which he had grown, was of a different order from this acceptance of loyalty from another man's followers. The pattern of feudal chieftain was forming, and he was surprised by the degree of his own acquiescence – and even pleasure – in it. They shook hands with him, and introduced themselves in their turn. Joe Harris ... Jess Awkright ... Bill Riggs ... Andy Anderson ... Will Secombe ... Martin Foster.

The women did not shake hands. Their men pointed them out to him. Awkright said: 'My wife, Alice.' Riggs said: 'That's my wife, Sylvie.' Foster, a thin-faced greying man, pointed: 'My wife Hilda, and my daughter, Hildegard.'

Alf Parson said: 'The other's Joe Ashton's wife, Emily. I reckon she'll be all right when she's got over the shock. He never did treat her right.'

All the men of Joe Ashton's party had shaken hands.

The elderly man of the first party stood at John's elbow.

He said: 'Have you changed your mind, Mr Custance? Can we stay with your lot?'

John could see now how the feudal leader, his strength an over-plus, might have given his aid to the weak, as an act of simple vanity. After enthronement, the tones of the suppliant beggar were doubly sweet. It was a funny thing.

'You can stay,' he said. 'Here.' He tossed him the shot-gun which he had been holding. 'We've come by a gun after all.'

When Pirrie killed Joe Ashton, the children down by the wall had frozen into the immobility of watchfulness which had come to replace ordinary childish fear. But they had soon begun playing again. Now the new set of children drifted down towards them, and, after the briefest of introductions, joined in the playing.

'My name's Noah Blennitt, Mr Custance,' the elderly man said, 'and that's my son Arthur. Then there's my wife Iris, and her sister Nelly, my young daughter Barbara, and my married daughter Katie. Her husband was on the railway; he was down in the south when the trains stopped. We're all very much beholden to you, Mr Custance. We'll serve you well, every one of us.'

The woman he had referred to as Katie looked at John, anxiously and placatingly.

'Wouldn't it be a good idea for us all to have some tea? We've got a big can and plenty of tea and some dried milk, and there's water in the brook just along.'

'It would be a good idea,' John said, 'if there were two dry sticks within twenty miles.'

She looked at him, shy triumph rising above the anxiety and the desire to please.

'That's all right, Mr Custance. We've got a primus stove in the pram as well.'

'Then go ahead. We'll have afternoon tea before we move off.' He glanced at the body of Joe Ashton. 'But somebody had better clear that away first.'

Two of Joe Ashton's erstwhile followers hastened to do his bidding.

TEN

PIRRIE walked with John for a time when they set out again; Jane, at a gesture from Pirrie, walked a demure ten paces in the rear. John had taken, as Joe Ashton had done, the head of the column, which now ran to the impressive number of thirty-four – a dozen men, a dozen women, and ten children. John had appointed four men to accompany him at the head of the column and five to go with Roger at the rear. In the case of Pirrie, he had made specific his roving commission. He could travel as he chose.

As they went down the road into the valley, separated somewhat from the other men, John said to him:

'It turned out very well. But it was taking a bit of a chance.'

Pirrie shook his head. 'I don't think so. It would have been taking a chance not to have killed him – and a rather long one. Even if he could have been persuaded to let you run things, he could not have been trusted.'

John glanced at him. 'Was it essential that I should run things? After all, the only important thing is getting to Blind Gill.'

'That is the most important thing, it is true, but I don't think we should ignore the question of what happens after we get there.'

'After we get there?'

Pirrie smiled. 'Your little valley may be peaceful and secluded, but it will have defences to man, even if relatively minor ones. It will be under siege, in other words. So there must be something like martial law, and someone to dispense it.'

'I don't see why. Some sort of committee, I suppose, with elected members, to make decisions ... surely that will be enough?'

'I think,' Pirrie said, 'that the day of the committee is over.'

His words echoed the thoughts that John himself had felt a short while before; for that reason, he replied with a forcefulness that had some anger in it:

'And the day of the baronn is back again? Only if we lose faith in our own ability to cope with things democratically.'

'Do you think so, Mr Custance?' Pirrie stressed the 'Mr' slightly, making it clear that he had noticed that, following the killing of Joe Ashton, the expression had somehow become a title. Except to Ann, and Roger and Olivia, John had now become Mr Custance; the others were known either by Christian names or surnames. It was a small thing, but not insignificant. Would Davey, John wondered, be Mr in his turn, by right of succession? The straying thought annoyed him.

He said curtly: 'Even if there has to be one person in charge of things at the valley, that one will be my brother. It's his land, and he's the most competent person to look after it.'

Pirrie raised his hands in a small gesture of mock resignation. 'Exit the committee,' he said, 'unlamented. That is another reason why you must be in charge of the party that reaches Blind Gill. Someone else might be less inclined to see that point.'

They moved down into the valley, passing the signs of destruction, which had been evident from higher up but which here were underlined in brutal scoring. What refugees there were avoided them; they had no temptation to look to an armed band for help. Near the ruins of Sedbergh they saw a group, of about the same number as their own, emerging from the town. The women were wearing what looked like expensive jewellery, and one of the men was carrying pieces of gold plate. Even while John watched, he threw some of it away as being too heavy. Another man picked it up, weighed it in his hand, and dropped it again with a laugh. They went on, keeping to the east of John's band, and the gold remained, gleaming dully against the brown grassless earth.

From an isolated farm-house, as they struck up towards the valley of the Lune, they heard a screaming, high-pitched and continuous, that unsettled the children and some of the women. There were two or three men lounging outside the farm-house with guns. John led his band past, and the screams faded into the distance.

The Blennitts' perambulator had been abandoned when they

left the road on the outskirts of Sedburgh, and their belongings distributed among the six adults in awkward bundles. The going was clearly harder for them than for any of the others, and they made no secret of their relief when John called a halt for the day, high up in the Lune valley, on the edge of the moors. The rain had not returned; the clouds had thinned into cirrus, threading the sky at a considerable height. Above the high curves of the moors to westward, the threads were lit from behind by the evening sun.

'We'll tackle the moors in the morning,' John said. 'By my reckoning, we aren't much more than twenty-five miles from the valley now, but the going won't be very easy. Still, I hope we can make it by tomorrow night. For tonight – he gestured towards a house with shattered windows that stood on a minor elevation above them – ' ... that looks like a promising billet. Pirrie, take a couple of men and reconnoitre it, will you?'

Pirrie, without hesitation, singled out Alf Parsons and Bill Riggs, and they accepted his selection with only a glance for confirmation at John. The three men moved up towards the house. When they were some twenty yards away, Pirrie waved them down into the cover of a shallow dip. Taking leisurely aim, he himself put a shot through an upstairs window. They heard the noise of the rifle, and the tiny splintering of glass. Silence followed.

A minute later, the small figure of Pirrie rose and walked towards the house. Apart from the rifle hunched under his arm, he had the air of a Civil Service official making a perfunctory business call. He reached the door, which apparently he found to be ajar, and kicked it open with his right foot. Then he disappeared inside.

Once again John was brought up sharp with the realization of how formidable an opponent Pirrie would have been had his ambition been towards the conscious exercise of power, instead of its promotion in another. He was walking now, alone, into a house which he could only guess to be empty. If he had any nerves at all, it was difficult to envisage a situation in which they would be drawn taut.

From an upper window, a face appeared – Pirrie's face – and

was withdrawn again. They waited, and at last he came out of the front door. He walked back down the path, sedately, and the two men rose and joined him. He came back to where John was.

John asked him: 'Well? O.K.?'

'Everything satisfactory. Not even bodies to dispose of. The people must have cleared off before the looters arrived.'

'It has been looted?'

'After a fashion. Not very professionally.'

'It will give us a roof for the night,' John said. 'What beds there are will do for the children. The rest of us can manage on the floor.'

Pirrie looked round him in speculation. 'Thirty-four. It isn't a very big house. I think Jane and I will risk the inclemency of the weather.' He nodded, and she came towards him, her rather stupid country face still showing no signs of anything but submission in the inevitable. Pirrie took her arm. He smiled. 'Yes, I think we will.'

'Just as you like,' John said. 'You can have a night off guard duty.'

'Thank you,' Pirrie said. 'Thank you, Mr Custance.'

John found a room in the upper storey which had two small beds in it, and he called up Davey and Mary to try them. There was a bathroom along the landing, with water still running, and he sent them there with instructions to wash. When they had gone, he sat on a bed, gazing out of the window, which looked down the valley towards Sedbergh. A magnificent view. Whoever lived here had probably been very attached to it – an indication, if such were needed, that immaterial possessions were as insecure as material ones.

His brief musing was interrupted by Ann's entry into the room. She looked tired. John indicated the other bed.

'Rest yourself,' he said. 'I've sent the kids along to smarten themselves up.'

She stood, instead, by the window, looking out.

'All the women asking me questions,' she said. 'Which meat shall we have tonight? . . . Can we use the potatoes up and rely on getting more tomorrow? . . . shall we cook them in their jackets or peel them first? . . . why me?'

He looked at her. 'Why not?'

'Because if you like being lord and master, it doesn't mean that I want to be the mistress.'

'You walked out on them, then?'

'I told them to put all their questions to Olivia.'

John smiled. 'Delegating responsibility, as a good mistress should.'

She paused; then said: 'Was it all necessary – joining up with these people, making ourselves into an army?'

He shook his head. 'No, not all. The Blennitts certainly not – but you wanted them, didn't you?'

'I didn't *want* them. It was just horrible, leaving the children. And I didn't mean them – I meant the others.'

'With the Blennitts – just the Blennitts – the odds would have tipped further against our getting through to the valley. With these others, we're going to make it easily.'

'Led by General Custance. And with the able assistance of his chief killer, Pirrie.'

'You underestimate Pirrie if you think he's just a killer.'

'No. I don't care how wonderful he is. He is a killer, and I don't like him.'

'I'm a killer, too.' He glanced at her. 'A lot of people are, who never thought they would be.'

'I don't need reminding. Pirrie's different.'

John shrugged. 'We need him – until we get to Blind Gill.'

'Don't keep saying that!'

'It's true.'

'John.' Their eyes met. 'It's the way he's changing you that's so dreadful. Making you into a kind of gangster boss – the children are beginning to be scared of you.'

He said grimly: 'If anything has changed me, it's been something more impersonal than Pirrie – the kind of life we have to lead. I'm going to get us to safety, all of us, and nothing is going to stop me. I wonder if you realize how well we've done to get as far as this? This afternoon, with the valley like a battlefield – that's only a skirmish compared with what's happening in the south. We've come so far, and we can see the rest of the way clear. But we can't relax until we're there.'

'And when we get there?'

He said patiently: 'I've told you – we can learn to live normally again. You don't imagine I like all this, do you?'

'I don't know.' She looked away, staring out of the window. 'Where's Roger?'

'Roger? I don't know.'

'He and Olivia have had to carry Steve between them since you've been so busy leading. They dropped behind. The only place left for them to sleep, by the time they got to the house, was the scullery.'

'Why didn't he come and see me?'

'He didn't want to bother you. When you called Davey up, Spooks stayed behind. He didn't think of coming with him, and Davey didn't think of asking. That's what I meant about the children becoming scared of you.'

John did not answer her. He went out of the room and called down from the landing:

'Rodge! Come on up, old man. And Olivia and the kids, of course.'

Behind him, Ann said, 'You're condescending now. I don't say you can help it.'

He went to her and caught her arms fiercely.

'Tomorrow evening, all this will be over. I'll hand things over to Dave, and settle down to learning from him how to be a potato and beef farmer. You will see me turn into a dull, yawning, clay-fingered old man – will that do?'

'If I could believe it will be like that ...'

He kissed her. 'It will be.'

Roger came in, with Steve and Spooks close behind him.

He said: 'Olivia's coming up, Johnny.'

'What the hell were you doing settling in the scullery?' John asked. 'There's plenty of room in here. We can put those beds together and get all the kids on them. For the rest of us, it's a nice soft floor. Fairly new carpets in the bedrooms – our hosts must have been on the luxurious side. There are blankets in that cupboard over there.'

Even while he spoke, he recognized his tone as being too hearty, with the bluffness of a man putting inferiors at their ease. But there was no way of changing it. The relationship between himself and Roger had changed on both sides, and it was beyond the power of them to return to the old common ground.

Roger said: 'That's very friendly of you, Johnny. The scullery was all very nice, but it had a smell of cockroaches. You two, you can cut along and line up for the bathroom.'

From the window Ann said: 'There they go.'

'They?' John asked. 'Who?'

'Pirrie and Jane – taking a stroll before dinner, I imagine.'

Olivia had come into the room while Ann was talking. She started to say something and then, glancing at John, stopped. Roger said:

'Pirrie the Wooer. Very sprightly for his age.'

Ann said to Olivia: 'You're looking after the knives. See that Jane gets a sharp one when she comes in to supper, and tell her there's no hurry to return it.'

'No!' The incisiveness had been involuntary; John moderated his voice: 'We need Pirrie. The girl's lucky to get him. She's lucky to be alive at all.'

'I thought we could see our way now,' Ann said. 'I thought tomorrow evening would see things back to normal. Do you really want Pirrie because he is essential to our safety, or have you grown to like him for yourself?'

'I told you,' John said wearily. 'I don't believe in taking any chances. Perhaps we won't need Pirrie tomorrow, but that doesn't mean that I take cheerfully to the idea of your egging the girl on to cut his throat during the night.'

'She may try,' Roger observed, 'of her own accord.'

'If she does,' Ann asked, 'what will you do, John – have her executed for high treason?'

'No. Leave her behind.'

Ann stared at him. 'I think you would!'

Speaking for the first time, Olivia said: 'He killed Millicent.'

'And we didn't leave him behind?' With exasperation, John went on: 'Can't you see that fair shares and justice don't work until you've got the walls to keep the barbarians out? Pirrie is more use than any one of us. Jane is like the Blennitts – a passenger, a drag. She can stay as long as she's careful how she walks, but no longer.'

Ann said: 'He really is a leader. Note the sense of dedication, most striking in the conviction that what he thinks is right because he thinks it.'

John said hotly: 'It's right in itself. Can you find an argument to refute it?'

'No.' She looked at him. 'Not one that you would appreciate.'

'Rodge!' He appealed to him. 'You see the sense in it, don't you?'

'Yes, I see the sense.' Almost apologetically, he added: 'I see the sense in what Ann says, too. I'm not blaming you for it, Johnny. You've taken on the job of getting us through, and you have to put that first. And it's Pirrie who's turned out to be the one you could rely on.'

He was about to reply argumentatively when he caught sight of their three faces, and memory was evoked by the way they were grouped. Some time in the past they had been in much the same positions – at the seaside, perhaps, or at a bridge evening. The recollection touched in him the realization of who he was and who they were – Ann, his wife, and Roger and Olivia, his closest friends.

He hesitated, then he said:

'Yes. I think I see it, too. Look – Pirrie doesn't matter a damn to me.'

'I think he does,' Roger said. 'Getting through matters to you, and so Pirrie does. It's not just his usefulness. Once again, Johnny, I'm not criticizing. I couldn't have handled the situation, because I wouldn't have had the stamina for it. But if I had been capable of handling it, I would have felt the same way about Pirrie.'

There was a pause before John replied.

'The sooner we get there the better,' he said. 'It will be nice to become normal again.'

Olivia looked at him, her shy eyes inquiring in her large placid face. 'Are you sure you will want to, Johnny?'

'Yes. Quite sure. But if we had another month of this, instead of another day to face, I wouldn't be so sure.'

Ann said: 'We've done beastly things. Some of us more so than others, perhaps, but all of us to some extent – if only by accepting what Pirrie's given us. I wonder if we ever can turn our backs on them.'

'We're over the worst,' John said. 'The going's plain and easy now.'

Mary and Davey came running in from the bathroom. They were laughing and shouting; too noisily.

John said: 'Quiet, you two.'

He had not, he thought, spoken any differently from his custom. In the past, the admonition would have had little if any effect. Now both fell quiet, and stood watching him. Ann, and Roger and Olivia, were watching him, too.

He bent towards Davey. 'Tomorrow night we should be at Uncle David's. Won't that be good, eh?'

Davey said: 'Yes, Daddy.'

The tone was enthusiastic enough, but the enthusiasm was tempered by an undue dutifulness.

In the early hours of the morning, John was awakened by a rifle shot and, as he sat up, heard it replied to from somewhere outside. He sat up, reaching for his revolver, and called to Roger, hearing him grunt something in reply.

Ann said: 'What's that?'

'Nothing much, probably. A stroller, hoping for easy pickings, maybe. You and Olivia stay here and see to the children. We'll go and have a look.'

The sentry's duty was to patrol outside the house, but he found Joe Harris, whose turn it was, staring out of a front room window on the ground floor. He was a thin dark man, with a heavy stubble of beard. His eyes gleamed in the moonlight, which shone into the house here.

'What's happening?' John asked him.

'I seen 'em when I was outside,' Harris said. 'Comin' up the valley from Sedburgh way. I figured it might be best not to disturb 'em in case they was going right on up the valley, so

I came on back into the house, and kept a watch from here.'

'Well?'

'They turned up towards the house. When I was certain they was coming this way, I had a crack at the bloke in front.'

'Did you hit him?'

'No. I don't think so. Another one had a shot back, and then they went down among the shrubs. They're still out there, Mr Custance.'

'How many?'

'It's hard to say, in this light. Might have been a dozen – maybe more.'

'As many as that?'

'That's why I was hoping they would go right through.'

John called: 'Rodge!'

'Yes.' Roger was standing at the door of the room. There were others in the room as well, but they were keeping quiet.

'Are the others up?'

'Three or four out here in the hall.'

Noah Blennitt's voice came from close behind John.

'Me and Arthur's here, Mr Custance.'

John said to Roger: 'Send one of them up to the back bedroom window to keep an eye open in case they try to work round that way. Then two each in the front bedrooms. Noah, you can take up your place at the other ground-floor window. I'll give you time to get into position. Then when I shout we'll let them have a volley. It may impress them enough to make them clear off. If it doesn't, pick your own targets after that. We have the territorial advantage. Women and kids well away from the windows, of course.'

He heard them moving away, as Roger relayed the instructions to them. In the room beside him a child's voice began to cry – Bessie Blennitt. He looked and saw her sitting up in an improvised bed; her mother was beside her, hushing her.

'I should take her round to the back,' he said. 'It won't be so noisy there.'

His own mildness surprised him. Katie Blennittt said:

'Yes, I'll take her, Mr Custance. You come along, too, Wilf. You'll be all right. Mr Custance is going to look after you.'

To the other woman, he said: 'You might as well all go to the back of the house.'

He knelt beside Joe Harris. 'Any sign of them moving yet?'

'I thought I saw summat. The shadows play you up.'

John stared out into the moonlit garden. There was no trace of cloud in a sky which was heavy with stars – fate playing tricks on both sides. The moonlight gave the defenders a considerable advantage, but if the cloud had held, the maurauders would probably have missed seeing the house, standing as it did apart and on a rise, altogether.

He thought a shadow moved, and then knew one did, not more than fifteen yards from the house. He cried very loudly:

'Now!'

Although he did not rate his chances of hitting anything with a revolver as very high, he took aim on the shadow that had moved, and fired through the open window. The volley that accompanied his shot was ragged but not unimpressive. He heard a cry of pain, and a figure spun round and fell awkwardly. John ducked to the side of the window in anticipation of the reply. There was a single shot, which seemed to splinter against the brickwork. After that, he could hear only a mumble of voices, and groaning from the man who had been hit.

The weight of fire-power must have come as an unpleasant surprise to them. They could not have expected an isolated house such as this to be held in force. Putting himself in the position of their leader, John reflected that his own concern, on stumbling on this kind of opposition, would have been to get his men out of the way with the least possible delay.

On the other hand, still retaining that viewpoint, he could see that there were snags. The moonlight certainly aided the defenders; and it was sufficiently bright to make good targets out of the attackers if they attempted any sudden disengagement. John peered up into the night sky, looking for cloud. If the moon were going to be obscured, it would be common sense for them to wait for it. But stars sparkled everywhere.

A further consideration must be that if the defenders could be overcome, the attackers stood to make a neat haul of arms, and possibly ammunition. Guns were worth taking risks for. And it was very probable that they had the advantage both in men and weapons.

It occurred to him that his show of force could have been tactically an error. Two or three rounds, instead of seven, might have been more likely to put them on the retreat. Pirrie might . . . Pirrie, he remembered, was somewhere outside, enjoying his nuptials.

The children must have all awoken by now, but they remained quiet. He heard someone coming downstairs. Roger called to him softly:

'Johnny!'

He kept his eyes on the garden. 'Yes.'

'What next?' There's one fellow standing out like a sore thumb from up there. Can we start knocking them off, or do you want to give them a chance to blow?'

He was reluctant to be the one to open the firing again. They knew his strength now. Further firing would be an expenditure of valuable ammunition with no prospect of any practical benefits.

'Wait,' he said. 'Give it a little longer.'

Roger said: 'Do you think . . . ?'

In the moonlight a shout rose: 'Gi'e it 'em!' John ducked automatically as a volley of shots slammed against the house with a shivering protesting crash of splintered glass. From above he heard one of his own men reply.

He called to Roger: 'All right. Get back upstairs, and tell them to use their discretion. If that gang change their minds and decide to pull out, let them go.'

This time one of the children had begun to cry, a frightened piercing wail. John felt far from optimistic as to the prospects of the attackers pulling out. They had presumably weighed the considerations as he had done, and decided their best chance lay in pressing the attack home.

While the new lull held, he called out into the garden:

'We don't want any trouble. We'll hold our fire if you clear off.'

He had taken the precaution of first flattening himself against the wall beside the window. Two or three shots thumped against the far wall of the room in answer. A man laughed, and he fired the revolver in the direction of the laugh. There was a rattle of sporadic fire, either way.

Watching intently, he saw a figure heave up out of the shadows, and fired again. Something sailed through the air, hit the side of the house, and dropped, not far from the window at which he and Joe Harris stood.

He shouted: 'Down, Joe!'

The explosion shattered what glass was left in the window panes, but did no other damage. A rattle of fire issued from the house.

Grenades, he thought sickly – why had the possibility not occurred to him? A fair portion of the guns that were now scattered throughout the countryside had originated in army barracks, and grenades were obviously as useful. For that matter, the men themselves had very possibly been soldiers; their present unconcern had a professional air to it.

Without any doubt, grenades tipped the scales against the defenders. A few more might miss, as the first had done, but eventually they would get them into the house, silencing the rooms one by one. The situation had suddenly changed its aspect. With the valley so close, he was facing defeat, and death, almost certainly, for all of them.

He said urgently to Joe Harris: 'Get upstairs and tell them to keep as continuous a fire on as they can. But aiming – not popping off wildly. As soon as they see someone lift his arm, slam everything at him. If we don't keep the grenades out, we've had it.'

Joe said: 'Right, Mr Custance.'

He did not seem particularly worried; either because he lacked the imagination to see what the grenades meant, or possibly owing to his faith in John's leadership. Pirrie had done a good job in that respect, but John would have exchanged it for Pirrie beside him in the house. If any of the others scored a hit, under these conditions, it would be by a fluke; Pirrie would have picked off the vague moonlit shadows without much difficulty.

John fired again at a movement, and his shot was reinforced

by shots from upstairs. Then from outside there was a swift concentrated burst directed towards one of the bedroom windows. Simultaneously, from another part of the garden, an arm rose, and a second grenade was lobbed through the air. It hit the side of the house again, and went off harmlessly. John fired at the point from which it had been thrown. There was a scatter of shots in different directions. In their wake came a cry which cut off half-way. The cry was from the garden. Someone had claimed another of the attackers.

It was encouraging, but no more than that. It made little difference to the probabilities of the outcome. John fired another round, and dodged sideways as a shot crashed past him in reply. The people outside were not likely to be discouraged by a lucky shot or two from the house finding their marks.

Even when, after a further interchange of shots, he saw a grenade arm rise again, and then saw it slump back with the grenade unthrown, he could only see the incident as a cause for grim satisfaction – not for hope. Two seconds later, the grenade went off, and set off a riot of explosion that made it abundantly clear that whoever held it had been carrying other grenades as well. There were shouts from that part of the garden, and some cries of pain. John fired into the noise, and the others followed suit. This time there was no answer.

All the same, it was with both astonishment and relief that John saw figures detach themselves from the cover of the ground and run, keeping as low as possible, away down the slope towards the valley. He fired after them, as the others did, and tried to number them as they retreated. Anything between ten and twenty – and with one, possibly two or three, left behind.

Everyone came crowding into the room – the women and children along with the men. In the dim light, John could see their faces, relieved and happy. They were all chattering. He had to speak loudly to make himself heard:

'Joe! You've got another half-hour on guard. We're doubling up for the rest of the night. You're on with him now, Noah. Jess will go with Roger afterwards, and Andy with Alf. I'll take a turn myself with Will. And from now on, raise the alarm first – and start wondering what it might be afterwards.'

Joe Harris said: 'You see, Mr Custance, I was hoping they would go on past.'

'Yes, I know,' John said. 'The rest of us might as well get back to bed.'

Alf Parsons asked: 'Any sign of Pirrie and his woman?'

He heard Olivia's voice: 'Jane – out there . . . '

'They will turn up,' he said. 'Go on back to bed now.'

'If that lot fell over them, they won't be turning up,' Parsons said.

John went to the window. He called: 'Pirrie! Jane!'

They listened in silence. There was no sound from outside. The moonlight lay like a summer frost on the garden.

'Should we go and have a look for them?' Parsons asked.

'No.' John spoke decisively. 'Nobody's moving out of here to-night. For one thing, we don't know how far those boys with the grenades have gone, or whether they have gone for good. Off to bed now. Let's get out of this room first, and give the Blennitts a chance. Come on. We need to rest ourselves ready for to-morrow.'

They dispersed quietly, though with some reluctance. John walked upstairs with Roger, following behind Ann and Olivia and the children. He went into the upstairs cloakroom, and Roger waited for him on the landing.

Roger said: 'I thought we'd had it for a time.'

'The grenades? Yes.'

'In fact, I think we were a bit lucky.'

'I don't quite understand it. We were certainly lucky dropping that bloke while he still had the grenades. That must have shaken them quite a bit. But I'm surprised that it shook them enough to make them pack things in. I didn't think they would.'

Roger yawned. 'Anyway, they did. What do you think about Pirrie and Jane?'

'Either they had gone far enough away to be out of earshot, or else they were spotted and bought it. Those people weren't bad shots. Not being in the house, they wouldn't have had any protection.'

'They could have drifted out of earshot.' Roger laughed. 'Along the paths of love.'

'Out of earshot of that racket? That would have brought Pirrie back.'

'There is another possibility,' Roger suggested. 'Jane may have tucked a knife in her garter on her own account. These ideas probably do occur to women spontaneously.'

'Where's Jane, then?'

'She still might have run across our friends. Or she might have tumbled to the fact that she would be less than popular here if she came back with a story of having mislaid her new husband on her bridal night.'

'She's got enough sense to know a woman's helpless on her own now.'

'Funny creatures, women,' Roger said. 'Ninety-nine times out of a hundred, they do the sensible thing without hesitation. The hundredth time they do the other with the same enthusiasm.'

John said curiously: 'You seem cheerful tonight, Rodge.'

'Who wouldn't be, after a reprieve like that? That second grenade came within a couple of feet of pitching in at my window.'

'And you won't be sorry if Pirrie has bought it, either from Jane or the grenade merchants.'

'Not particularly. Not at all, in fact. I think I'd be rather pleased, I told you – there's been no need for me to get myself fixated on Pirrie. I haven't had to run things.'

'Is that what you would call it – fixated?'

'You don't find many Pirrie's about. The pearl in the oyster – hard and shining and, as far as the oyster is concerned, a disease.'

'And the oyster?' John offered ironically: 'The world as we know it.'

'The analogy's too complicated. I'm tired as well. But you know what I mean about Pirrie. In abnormal conditions, invaluable; but I hope to God we aren't going to live in those conditions for ever.'

'He was a peaceable enough citizen before. There's no reason to think he wouldn't have been once again.'

'Isn't there? You can't put a pearl back inside the oyster. I wasn't looking forward to life in the valley with Pirrie standing just behind you, ready to jog your elbow.'

'In the valley, David's boss, if anyone has to be. Not me, not Pirrie. You know that.'

'I've never met your brother,' Roger said. 'I know very little about him. But he hasn't had to bring his family and hangers-on through a world that breaks up as you touch it.'

'That doesn't make any difference.'

'No?' Roger yawned again. 'I'm tired. You turn in. It's not worth my while for half an hour. I'll just look in and see that the kids have bedded down.'

They stood together in the doorway of the room. Ann and Olivia were lying on blankets under the window; Ann looked up as she saw them standing there, but did not say anything. A shaft of moonlight extended to the double bed that had been created out of the two single ones. Mary lay curled up by the wall. Davey and Steve were snuggled in together, with one of Davey's arms thrown across Steve's shoulder. Spooks, his features strangely adult without his spectacles, was at the other side. He was awake also, staring up at the ceiling.

'Don't think I'm not grateful for Pirrie,' Roger said. 'But I'm glad we've found we can manage without him.'

In the new pattern of life, the hours of sleep were from nine to four, the children being packed off, when possible, an hour earlier, and sleeping on after the others until breakfast was ready. It began to be light during the last watch, which John shared with Will Secombe. He went out into the garden and examined the field of the skirmish. There was a man about twenty-five, shot through the side of the head, about fifteen yards from the house. He was wearing army uniform and had a jewelled brooch pinned on his chest. If the stones were diamond, as they appeared to be, it must have been worth several hundred pounds at one time.

There were tatters of army uniform on the other body in the garden. This one was a considerably more ugly sight; he had apparently been carrying grenades round his waist, and the first one had set them off. It was difficult to make out anything of what he had been like in life. John called Secombe, and they dragged both bodies well away from the house and shoved them out of sight under a clump of low-lying holly.

Secombe was a fair-haired, fair-skinned man; he was in his middle thirties but looked a good deal younger. He kicked a protruding leg farther under the holly, and looked at his hands with disgust.

John said: 'Go in and have a wash, if you like. I'll look after things. It will be time for reveille soon, anyway.'

'Thanks, Mr Custance. Nasty job, that. I didn't see anything as bad as that during the war.'

When he had gone, John had another look round the environs of the house. The man who had had the grenades had had a rifle as well; it lay where he had lain, bent and useless. There was no sign of any other weapon; that belonging to the other corpse had presumably been taken away in the retreat.

He found nothing else, apart from two or three cartridge clips and a number of spent cartridge cases. He was looking for signs of Pirrie or Jane, but there was nothing. In the dawn light, the valley stretched away, without sign of life. The sky was still clear. It looked like a good day lying ahead.

He thought of calling again, and then decided it would be useless. Secombe came back out of the house, and John looked at his watch.

'All right. You can get them up now.'

Breakfast was almost ready and there were sounds of the children moving about when John heard Roger exclaim:

'Good God!'

They were in the front room from which John had directed operations during the night. John followed Roger's gaze out of the shattered window. Pirrie was coming up the garden path, his rifle under his arm; Jane walked just behind him.

John called to him: 'Pirrie! What the hell have you been up to?'

Pirrie smiled slightly. 'Would you not regard that as a delicate question?' He nodded towards the garden. 'You cleared the mess up, then?'

'You heard it?'

'It would have been difficult not to. Did they land either of the grenades inside?' John shook his head. 'I thought not.'

'They cleared off when things were beginning to get hot,' John said. 'I'm still surprised about that.'

'The side fire probably upset them,' Pirrie said.

'Side fire?'

Pirrie gestured to where, on the right of the house, the ground rose fairly steeply.

John said: 'You were having a go at them – from there?'

Pirrie nodded. 'Of course.'

'Of course,' John echoed. 'That explains a few things. I was wondering who we had in the house who could hit that kind of target in that kind of light, and kill instead of just wounding.' He looked at Pirrie. 'Then you heard me call you, after they had cleared off? Why didn't you give me a hail back?'

Pirrie smiled again. 'I was busy.'

They travelled easily and uneventfully that day, if fairly slowly. Their route now lay for the most part across the moors, and there were several places where it was necessary to leave the roads and cut over the bare or heathery slopes, or to follow by the side of one of the many rivers or streams that flowed down from the moors into the dales. The sun rose at their backs into a cloudless sky, and before midday it was too hot for comfort. John called an early halt for dinner, and afterwards told the women to get the children down to rest in the shade of a group of sycamores.

Roger asked him: 'Not pressing on with all speed?'

He shook his head. 'We're within reach now. We'll be there before dark, which is all that matters. The kids are fagged out.'

Roger said: 'So am I.' He lay back on the dry, stony ground, and rested his head on his hands. 'Pirrie isn't, though.'

Pirrie was explaining something to Jane, pointing out over the flat lands to the south.

'She won't knife him now,' Roger added. 'Another Sabine woman come home to roost. I wonder what the little Pirries will be like?'

'Millicent didn't have any children.'

'Conceivably Pirrie's fault, but more probably Millicent's. She was the kind of woman who would take care not to be burdened with kids. They would spoil her chances.'

'Millicent seems a long time ago,' John said.

'The relativity of time. How long since I found you up in your crane? It seems something like six months.'

The moors had been more or less deserted, but when they descended to cross the lower land north of Kendal, they witnessed the signs, by now familiar, of the predatory animal that man had become: houses burning, an occasional cry in the distance that might be either of distress or savage exultance, the sights and sounds of murder. And another of their senses was touched – here and there their nostrils were pricked by the sour-sweet smell of flesh in corruption.

But their own course was not interrupted, and soon they began to climb again, up the bare bleak bones of the moors towards their refuge. Skylarks and meadow pipits could be heard in the empty arching sky, and for a time a wheatear ran along ahead of them, a few paces in front. Once they sighted a deer, about three hundred yards off. Pirrie dropped to the ground to take careful aim on it, but it darted away behind a shoulder of the moor before he could fire. Even from that distance it looked emaciated. John wondered on what diet it had been surviving. Mosses, possibly, and similar plants.

It was about five o'clock when they came to the waters of the Lepe. It tumbled with the same swift urgency of pace that it had always had; here its course lay between rocky banks so that not even the absence of grass detracted from the evocation of its familiarity.

Ann stood beside John. She looked more calm and happier than she had done since they left London.

'Home,' she said, 'at last.'

'About two miles,' John said. 'But we'll see the gateway in less than a mile. I know the river for several miles farther down. And a bit farther up you can get into the middle of the river, on stepping-stones. Dave and I used to fish from there.'

'Are there fish in the Lepe? I didn't know.'

He shook his head. 'We never caught any inside the valley. I don't think they travel so far up. But down here there are trout.' He smiled. 'We'll send expeditions out and net them. We must have some variety in our diet.'

She smiled back. 'Yes. Darling, I think I can really believe it now – that everything's going to be all right – that we're going to be happy and human again.'

'Of course. I never doubted it.'

'Dave's stockade,' John said. 'It looks nice and solid.'

They were in sight of the entrance to Blind Gill. The road squeezed in towards the river and the high timber fence ran from the water's edge across the road to the steeply rising hillside. That part which covered the road looked as though it might open to form a gate.

Pirrie had come forward to walk with John; he too surveyed the fence with respect.

'An excellent piece of work. Once we are on the other ...'

It was the crude anger of machine-gun fire that broke into his words. For a moment, John stood there, shocked. He called, more in bewilderment than anything else: 'Dave!'

There was a second burst of fire, and this time he ran to get Davey and Mary. He shouted to the others: 'Get into the ditch!' He saw that Mary was pulling Davey and Spooks down with her, and that Mary was already crouching in the ditch beside the road. He ran for it himself, and lay down beside them.

Mary said: 'What's happening, Daddy?'

'Where is it firing from?' Ann asked.

He pointed towards the fence. 'From there. Did everyone get clear? Who's that on the road? Pirrie!'

Pirrie's small body lay stretched across the camber of the road. There was blood underneath him.

Ann caught hold of John as he began to rise. 'No! You mustn't. Stay where you are. Think of the children – me.'

'I'll get him away,' he said. 'They won't fire while I'm getting him away.'

Ann held on to him. She was crying; she called to Mary, and Mary also grasped his coat. While he was trying to pull himself free, he saw that someone else had got up from the ditch and was running towards where Pirrie lay. It was a woman.

John stopped struggling, and said in amazement: 'Jane!'

Jane put her hands under Pirrie's shoulders and lifted him easily. She did not look at the fence where the gun was mounted.

She got one of his arms over her own shoulder and half dragged, half carried him to the ditch. She eased him down beside John and sat down herself, taking his head in her lap.

Ann asked: 'Is he – dead?'

Blood was pouring from the side of his head. John wiped it away. The wound, he could see at once, was only superficial. A bullet had grazed his skull, with enough force to knock him over. There was an abrasion on the other side of his head, where he had probably hit the ground. It was very likely the fall which had knocked him unconscious.

John said: 'He'll live.' Jane looked up; she was crying. 'Pass the word along to Olivia that we want the bandage,' John added. And a wad of lint.'

Ann stared from Pirrie to the fence barring the road. 'But why should they fire at us? What's happened?'

'A mistake.' John stared at the fence. 'A mistake – we'll sort it out easily enough.'

ELEVEN

ANN tried to stop him when she saw him tying a large white handkerchief on the end of a stick.

'You can't do that! They'll shoot you!'

John shook his head. 'No, they won't.'

'They fired on all of us without provocation. They'll fire at you, too.'

'Without provocation? A whole gang of us marching up the road, and with arms? It was as much my mistake as theirs. I should have realized how their minds would work.'

'Their minds? David's!'

'No. Probably not. He can hardly be manning the fence all the time. God knows who it is. Anyway, it's a different thing with one man, unarmed, under a flag of truce. There's no reason why they should fire.'

'But they might!'

'They won't.'

But he had an odd feeling as he walked along the middle of the road towards the fence, his white flag held above his head. It was not exactly fear. It seemed to him that it was nearer to exhilaration – the sense of fatigue allied to excitement that he had sometimes known in fevers. He began to measure his paces, counting soundlessly: one, two, three, four, five ... In front of him, he saw that the barrel of the machine-gun poked through a hole in the fence a good ten feet above the ground; not far from the top. David must have built a platform on the other side.

He stopped, seven or eight feet from the fence, and looked up. From somewhere near the gun muzzle, a voice said:

'Well, what are you after?'

John said: 'I'd like to have a word with David Custance.'

'Would you, now? He's busy. And the answer's no, anyway.'

'He's my brother.'

There was a moment's silence. Then the voice said:

'His brother's in London. Who do you say you are?'

'I'm John Custance. We got away from London. It's taken us some time to travel up here. Can I see him?'

'Wait a minute.' There was a low murmur of voices; John could not quite catch what was said. 'All right. You can wait there. We're sending up to the farm for him.'

John walked a few paces, and stared into the Lepe. From beyond the fence he heard a car engine start up and then fade away along the road up the valley. It sounded like David's utility. He wondered how much petrol they would have in store inside Blind Gill. Probably not much. It didn't matter. The sooner people got used to a world deprived of the internal combustion engine as well as the old-fashioned beasts of burden, the better.

He called up to the man behind the fence: 'The people with me – can they come out of the ditch? Without being shot at?'

'They can stay where they are.'

'But there's no point in it. What's the objection to their being on the road?'

'The ditch is good enough.'

John thought of arguing, and then decided against it. Anyone on the other side of the fence was someone they would have to live with; if this fellow wanted to exercise his brief authority, it was best to put up with it. His own disquiet had been allayed by the promptness with which it had been agreed to send for David. That at least removed the fear that he might have lost control of the valley.

He said: 'I'll walk along and tell my lot what's happening.'

The voice was indifferent. 'Please yourself. But keep them off the road.'

Pirrie was sitting up and taking notice now. He listened to what John had to tell them, but made no comment. Roger said:

'You think it's going to be all right, then?'

'I don't see why not. The bloke behind the machine gun may be a bit trigger-happy, but that won't bother us once we're behind him.'

'He don't seem very anxious to let us get behind him,' Alf Parsons said.

'Carrying out orders. Hello!'

There was the sound of an engine approaching. It halted behind the barrier.

'That will be David!' John got to his feet again. 'Ann, you could come along and have a word with him, too.'

'Isn't it a risk?' Roger asked.

'Hardly. David's there now.'

Ann said: 'Davey would like to come, too. I should think – and Mary.'

'Of course.'

Pirrie said 'No.' He spoke softly, but with finality. John looked at him.

'Why? What's wrong?'

'I think they would be safer here,' Pirrie said. He paused. 'I don't think you should all go along there together.'

It took several seconds for John to grasp the implication; he only did so then because the remark came from Pirrie and so could be founded only on an utterly cynical realism.

'Well,' he said at last, 'that tells me something about how you would act in my place, doesn't it?'

Pirrie smiled. Ann said: 'What's the matter?'

John heard David's voice calling him in the distance: 'John!' 'Nothing,' he said. 'Never mind, Ann. You stay here. It won't take me long to fix things with David.'

He had half expected the gate in the fence to open as he approached, but he realized that caution – possibly excessive, but on the whole justified – might prevent this until John's status, and the status of the troop that accompanied him, had been settled. He stood under the fence, still blind to whatever was happening on the other side of it, and said:

'Dave! That you?'

He heard David's voice: 'Yes, of course – open it. How the devil is he going to get in if you don't?'

He saw the muzzle of the gun waggle as the gate beneath it opened slightly. No chances were being taken. He squeezed through the gap, and saw David waiting for him. They took each other's hands. The gate closed behind him.

'How did you make it?' David asked. 'Where's Davey – and Ann and Mary?'

'Back there. Hiding in a ditch. Your machine-gunner damn near killed us all.'

David stared at him. 'I can't believe it! I told the people at the gate to look out for you, but I never believed you would get here. The news of the ban on travel ... and then the rioting and rumours of bombing ... I'd given you up.'

'It's a long story,' John said. 'It can wait. Can I bring my lot in first?'

'Your lot? You mean ... ? They told me there was a mob on the road.'

John nodded. 'A mob. Thirty-four of them, ten being children. We've all been on the road for some time. I brought them here.'

He was looking at David's face. He had seen the expression only once before that he could remember: when, after their grandfather's death, they had heard that the whole estate was being left to David. It showed guilt and embarrassment.

David said: 'It's a bit difficult, Johnny.'

'In what way?'

'We're crowded out already. When things began getting bad, the locals began to come in. The Rivers from Stonebeck, and so on. It was their boy who got hold of the machine-gun – from an army unit near Windermere. Three or four of the men came with him. It's spread thin. We'll manage all right, but there's no margin for accidents – a potato failure, or anything like that.'

'My thirty-four will spread it thinner,' John said. 'But they'll work for their keep. I'll answer for that.'

'That's not the point,' David said. 'The land will only support so many. We're over the mark now.'

A brief silence followed. The Lepe rushed past on their right. The man tending a fire on which a pot was simmering and the two men up on the platform were both out of earshot. Nevertheless, John found himself lowering his voice. He said:

'What do you suggest? That we turn back towards London?'

David grasped his arm. 'Good God, no! Don't be a fool. I'm trying to tell you – I can make room for you and Ann and the children; but not for the others.'

'Dave,' he said, 'you've got to make room for them. You can do, and you must.'

David shook his head. 'I would if I could. Don't you understand – those people aren't the first we've had to turn away. There have been others. Some of them were relations of people already here. We've had to be hard. I've always told them that you and your family must come in if you got here. But thirty-four ... ! It's impossible. Even if I agreed, the others would never let me.'

'It's your land.'

'No one holds land except by consent. They are in the majority. Johnny – I know you don't like the idea of abandoning the people you've been travelling with. But you will have to. There's no alternative.'

'There's always an alternative.'

'None. Bring them here – Ann and the children – you can make some excuse for that. The others ... they've got arms, haven't they? They'll manage all right.'

'You've not been out there.'

Their eyes met again. David said: 'I know you won't like doing it, but you must. You can't put the safety of those others before Ann and the children.'

John laughed. The two men on the platform looked down at them.

'Pirrie!' he said. 'He must be psychic.'

'Pirrie?'

'One of my lot. I don't think we should have got through without him. I was going to bring Ann and the children with me when I came to meet you. He put a stop to it. He made them stay behind. I saw that he was protecting himself and the others against a double-cross, and I was righteously indignant. Now ... if I did have them here, inside the fence, I wonder what I would have done?'

David said: 'This is serious. Can't you fool him somehow?'

'Fool him? Not Pirrie.' John looked away, up the long vista of Blind Gill, snug beneath its protecting hills. He said slowly: 'If you turn those others down, you're turning us down – you're turning Davey down.'

'This man, Pirrie. ... I might persuade them to let one other in with you. Can he be bribed?'

'Undoubtedly. But the idea will have entered the heads of the others by now – particularly since I shall have to tell them they can't just walk in as they had been hoping. There isn't a hope of my getting the children in here without them all coming.'

'There must be some way.'

'That's what I said to you, isn't it? We aren't free agents any longer, though.' He stared at his brother. 'In a way, we're enemies.'

'No. We'll find a way round this. Perhaps ... if you were to go back, and then I got our people to run a sortie against you, under machine-gun cover ... you could have passed the word to Ann and the children to lie still until we had chased them away.'

John smiled ironically. 'Even if I were prepared to do it, it wouldn't work. Mine have been blooded. That ditch makes a fair cover. The machine-gun isn't going to scare them.'

'Then ... I don't know. But there must be something.'

John looked up the valley again. The fields were well cropped, mostly with potatoes.

'Ann will be wondering,' he said, 'not to mention the others. I shall have to get back. What's it to be, Dave?'

He had come already to his own decision, and the agony of his brother's uncertainty could not touch that grimness. Dave said at last, forcing the words out:

'I'll talk to them. Come back in an hour. I'll see what they say about letting the others in. Or perhaps we'll think of something in that time. Try to think of something, Johnny!'

John nodded. 'I'll try. So long, Dave.'

David looked at him miserably: 'Give my love to them all – to Davey.'

John said: 'Yes, of course I will.'

The two men came down from the platform and unbarred the gate again. John squeezed through. He did not look at David as he went.

They were waiting for him as he dropped into the ditch. He saw from their faces that they expected only bad news; any news was bad that was not signalled by the gate to the valley thrown open, and an immediate beckoning in.

'How'd it go, Mr Custance?' Noah Blennitt asked.

'Not well.' He told them, baldly, but passing quickly over the invitation to his own family to come in. When he had finished, Roger said:

'I can see their point of view. He can make room for you and Ann and the children?'

'*He* can't do anything. The others had agreed about that, and apparently they're willing to stick by it.'

'You take it, Johnny,' Roger said. 'You've brought us up here – we haven't lost anything by it, and there's no sense in everyone missing the chance because we can't all have it.'

The murmur from the others was uncertain enough to be tempting. It's been offered, he thought, and they won't stop me if I take it straight away while they're still shocked by their own generosity. Take Ann and Mary and Davey up to the gates, and see them open, and the valley beyond. ... He looked at Pirrie. Pirrie returned the look calmly; his small right hand, the fingers still carefully manicured, rested on the butt of his rifle.

Seeing the bubble of temptation pricked, he wondered how he would have reacted if he had had the real rather than the apparent freedom of action. The feudal baron, he thought, and ready to sell out his followers as cheerfully as that. Probably they had been like that – most of them, anyway.

He said, looking at Pirrie: 'I've been thinking it over. Quite frankly, I don't think there's any hope at all of my brother persuading the others to let us all in. As he said, some of them have seen their own relations turned back. That leaves us two alternatives: turning back ourselves and looking for a home somewhere else, or fighting our way into the valley and taking it over.'

Ann said: 'No!' in a shocked voice. Davey said: 'Do you mean – fighting Uncle Dave, Daddy?' The others stayed silent.

'We don't have to decide straight away,' John said. 'Until I've seen my brother again, I suppose we can say there's an outside chance of managing it peaceably. But you can be thinking it over.'

Roger said: 'I still think you ought to take what's offered you, Johnny.'

This time there was no kind of response; the moment of

indecision past, John reflected wrily. The followers had realized the baron's duty towards them again.

Alf Parsons asked: 'What do you think, Mr Custance?'

'I'll keep my opinion until I come back next time,' John said. 'You be thinking it over.'

Pirrie still did not speak, but he smiled slowly. With the bandage round his head, he looked a frail and innocent old man. Jane sat close by him, her pose protective.

It was not until John was on the point of going back to the gate that Pirrie said anything. Then he said:

'You'll look things over, of course? From inside?'

'Of course,' John said.

If there had been any hope in his mind of David persuading the others in the valley to relent, it would have vanished the moment he saw his brother's face again. Four or five other men had accompanied him back to the fence, presumably to help the three already on guard in the event of John's troops being reluctant to accept their dismissal. There was, John noticed, a telephone point just inside the fence, so that the men there could summon help quickly in the event of a situation looking dangerous. He glanced about him, looking for further details of the valley's defences.

David said: 'They won't agree, Johnny. We couldn't really expect them to.'

The men who had come with him stayed close by, making no pretence of offering privacy to the brothers. As much as anything, this showed John the powerlessness of his brother's position.

He nodded. 'So we have to take the road again. I gave Davey your love. I'm sorry you couldn't have seen him.'

'Look,' David said, 'I've been thinking – there is a way.' He spoke with a feverish earnestness. 'You can do it.'

John looked at him in inquiry. He had been noting the angle the fence made with the river.

'Tell them it's no good,' David said, ' – that you will have to find somewhere else. But don't travel too far tonight. Arrange things so that you and Ann and the children can slip away – and then come back here. You'll be let in. I'll stay here tonight to make sure.'

John recognized the soundness of the scheme, for other people under other conditions. But he was not tempted by it. In any case, David was underestimating the intervention Pirrie might make in the plan; a reasonable error for anyone who did not know Pirrie.

He said slowly: 'Yes, I think that might work. It's worth trying, anyway. But I don't want to have the kids mown down by that gun of yours in the night.'

David said eagerly: 'There's no fear of that. Give me our old curlew whistle as you come along the road. And it's full moon.'

'Yes,' John said, 'so it is.'

TWELVE

JOHN dropped down into the ditch where they all were.

He said immediately: 'We shan't get in there peaceably. They won't budge. My brother's tried them, but it's no good. So we have the alternatives I spoke of – going somewhere else or fighting our way into Blind Gill. Have you thought about it?'

There was a silence; Alf Parsons broke it. He said:

'It's up to you, Mr Custance – you know that. We shall do whatever you think best.'

'Right,' John said. 'One thing first. My brother looks like me, and he's wearing blue overalls and a grey and white check shirt. I'm telling you this so you can watch out for him. I don't want him hurt, if it can be helped.'

Joe Harris said: 'We're having a go, then, Mr Custance?'

'Yes. Not now – tonight. Now we are going to beat an orderly retreat out of range of vision of the people on the fence. It's got to look as though we've given up the idea of getting in. Our only hope is having the advantage of surprise.'

They obeyed at once, scrambling out of the ditch and heading back down the road, away from the valley. John walked at the rear, and Roger and Pirrie walked with him.

Roger said: 'I still think you're doing the wrong thing, Johnny. You could leave us and take the family back. They would have you.'

Pirrie remarked, in a speculative tone: 'I don't think it's going to be easy, even a surprise attack.' He looked at John. 'Unless you know a way of getting in over the hills.'

'No. Even if there were a reasonable way, it wouldn't do. The hillsides are steep in there. It would be impossible to avoid starting small slides of stones and once they knew where we were we should offer a target they couldn't miss.'

'I take it,' Pirrie said, 'that you do not contemplate rushing that fence – with a Vickers machine-gun behind it?'

'No.' John looked at Pirrie closely. 'How do you feel now?'

'Normal.'

'Fit enough to wade half a mile through a river that's cold even at this time of year?'

'Yes.'

They were both watching him in inquiry. John said:

'My brother put a fence across the gap between hill and river, but he took it for granted the river was fence enough in itself. By the banks it's deep as well as swift – there have been enough cattle drowned in it, and quite a few men. But I fell in from the other side when I was a kid, and I didn't drown. There's a shelf just about the middle of the river – even as a boy of eleven I could stand there, with my head well above water.'

Roger asked: 'Are you suggesting we all wade up the river? They would see us, surely. And what about getting out of it, if it's as deep by the banks as you say?'

Pirrie, as John had anticipated, had grasped the idea without the need for elaboration.

'I am to knock out the machine gun?' he suggested. 'And the rest of you?'

'I'm coming with you,' John said. 'I'll take one of the other rifles. I'm not likely to succeed if you fail, but it provides us with an extra chance. Roger, you've got to take that fence once we've got the gun quiet. You can get the men up within a hundred yards of it, along the ditch. The fence is climbable.

'They will bring the gun round to bear on us as soon as they are under fire from the rear. That's when you take our lot in.'

Roger said doubtfully: 'Will it work?'

It was Pirrie who answered him. 'Yes,' he said, 'I believe it will.'

He stood with Ann, looking at the children as they lay asleep on the ground – Davey and Spooks and Steve tangled up together, and Mary a little apart, her head pillowed on an outthrust arm. He told her then, in an undertone, of David's plan. When he had finished, she said:

'Why didn't you? We could have done it. We could have got away from Pirrie somehow' – she shivered – 'killed him if necessary! There's been enough killing of innocent people – and now there's going to be more. Oh, why didn't you take it? Can't we still?'

The sun had gone down and the moon was yet to rise. It was quite dark. He could not see much of her face, nor she of his.

He said: 'I'm glad of Pirrie.'

'Glad!'

'Yes. I needed the thought of that trigger finger of his to stiffen me, but it only stiffened me into taking the right course. Ann, some of the things I've had to do to get us here have been nasty. I couldn't have justified them even to myself, except in the hope that it would all be different once we got to the valley.'

'It will be different.'

'I hope so. That's why I won't pay for admission in treachery.'

'Treachery?'

'To the rest of them.' He nodded his head towards the others. 'It would be treachery to abandon them now.'

'I don't understand.' Ann shook her head. 'I don't begin to understand. Isn't it treachery to David – to force a way in?'

'David isn't a free agent. If he were, he would have let us all in. You know that. Think, Ann! Leaving Roger and Olivia outside – and Steve and Spooks. What would you tell Davey? And all these other poor devils ... Jane ... yes, and Pirrie? However much you dislike him, we should have never got near the valley without him.'

Ann looked down at the sleeping children. 'All I can think is that we could have been safe in the valley tonight – without any fighting.'

'But with nasty memories.'

'We have those anyway.'

'Not in the same way.'

She paused for a while. 'You're the leader, aren't you? The medieval chieftain – you said so yourself?'

John shrugged. 'Does that matter?'

'It does to you. I see that now. More than our safety and the children's.'

He said gently: 'Ann, darling, what are you talking about?'

'Duty. That's it, isn't it? It wasn't really Roger and Olivia, Steve and Spooks, you were thinking about – not them as persons. It was your own honour – the honour of the chieftain. You aren't just a person yourself any longer. You're a figurehead as well.'

'Tomorrow it will be all over. We can forget about it all then.'

'No. You half convinced me before, but I know better now. You've changed and you can't change back.'

'I've not changed.'

'When you're King of Blind Gill,' she said, 'how long will it be, I wonder, before they make a crown for you?'

The risky part, John thought, was the stretch between the bend of the river and the point, some thirty yards from the fence, where the shadow of the hill cancelled out the moonlight. If they had left it until the moon was fully risen, the project would have been almost impossible, for the moonlight was brilliant and they had to pass within yards of the defenders.

As it was, they were exposed, for some twenty-five yards, to any close scrutiny that the people behind the fence turned on the river. The reasonable hope was that their attention would be focused on the obvious approach by road rather than the apparently impractical approach up so swift and deep a river as the Lepe. Pirrie, in front of him, crouched down so that only his head and shoulders, and one hand holding the rifle on his shoulder, were out of the water, and John followed suit.

The water was even colder than John remembered it as being, and the effort of struggling forward against the current was an exhausting one. Once or twice, Pirrie slipped, and he had to hold him. It was a consolation that the noise of the river would cloak any noise they might make.

They pushed ahead and at last, to their relief, found themselves clear of the moonlight. The hill's shadow was long but of no great width; they could see the moonlit road and the fence quite plainly. John had not been sure of this beforehand, and it raised his hopes still further. If the fence had been in shadow, even Pirrie's marksmanship might not have availed them.

When they were not more than ten yards from the fence, Pirrie stopped.

John whispered urgently: 'What is it?'

He heard Pirrie draw gasping breaths. 'I . . . exhausted . . .'

It was a shock to remember that Pirrie was an old man, and of frail physique, who had made a harassing journey and only a few hours before had been knocked over by a bullet. John braced himself and put his free arm round Pirrie's waist.

He said softly: 'Rest a minute. If it's too much for you, go back. I'll carry on by myself.'

They stayed like that for several seconds. Pirrie was shuddering against John's body. Then he pulled himself upright.

He gasped: 'All right now.'

'Are you sure?'

Making no answer, Pirrie waded on. They were abreast of the fence, and then beyond it.

John looked back. The valley's defences were outlined in the moon's soft radiance. There were three men on the platform, and another three or four huddled on the ground behind it, presumably asleep. He whispered to Pirrie:

'Here?'

'Give ourselves a chance,' said Pirrie. 'Lengthen the range ... I can hit them at another twenty yards. . . .'

His voice seemed stronger again. Pirrie was probably indestructible, John reflected. He trudged after him through the swirling water, aware of fatigue now in his own limbs, doubling the water's drag.

Pirrie stopped at last, and turned, bracing himself against the current. They were about twenty-five yards inside the valley. John stood at his left elbow.

'Try for the one on the right,' Pirrie said. 'I'll manage the other two.'

'The machine-gun first,' John said.

Pirrie did not bother to reply to that. He drew his rifle up to his shoulder, and John, more slowly, did the same.

Pirrie's rifle cracked viciously, and in the moonlight the figure of the man behind the machine-gun straightened up, cried in pain, and went down again, clutching at the edge of the platform and missing it. John fired for his own target, but did not hit. More surprisingly, Pirrie's second shot failed of its mark. Both men remaining on the platform raced for the machine-gun, and tried to swing it round. Pirrie fired again as they did so, and one of them slumped across it. The other pushed him free, and managed to turn it. John and Pirrie fired again unsuccessfully. The figures beneath the platform had risen and were reaching for guns. Then the machine-gun began to sputter in a staccato rhythm of sound and flame.

It did not manage much more than a dozen rounds before Pirrie got his third victim, and the deadly chatter stopped. The men on the ground had begun to fire at them now, but the whine of individual bullets seemed irrelevant.

Pirrie said: 'The ladder ... keep them off the platform ... '

His voice was weaker again, but John saw him re-load, and, with his usual snatched but unwavering aim, hit yet another figure, which had begun to climb the ladder to the platform. John tried to listen for sounds of Roger and the others beyond the fence, but could hear nothing. They must have reached the fence by now. He looked at the black line of the fence's top, searching for the figures that should be climbing over it.

Suddenly, in an entirely natural and unforced tone, Pirrie said:

'Take this.'

He was holding out his rifle.

John said: 'Why ... ?'

'You fool,' Pirrie said. 'I'm hit.'

A bullet whined towards them across the surface of the water. John could see, examining him closely, that his shirt was holed and bloody at the shoulder. He took the gun, dropping the one he had into the water.

'Hang on to me,' he told Pirrie.

'Never mind that. The ladder!'

There was another figure on the ladder. John fired, re-loaded, fired again. The third shot succeeded. He turned to Pirrie.

'Now ... ' he began.

But Pirrie was gone. John thought he saw his body, several yards downstream, but it was difficult to be sure. He looked back to the more important concern – the fence. Figures were swarming across the top, and one already had hold of the machine-gun, tilting it downwards.

He saw the remaining defenders throw their guns away and then, chilled and utterly tired, began looking for the best place to get in to the bank.

THIRTEEN

INTO this room he had come with David, side by side, their fingers locked together to calm each other's fear and uncertainty before the mystery of death, to see the corpse of Grandfather Beverley. The room had changed very little in a score of years. David had never had any desire to modernize his surroundings.

Ann said: 'Darling, I'm sorry – for what I said last night.' He did not answer. 'It is going to be different now. You were right.'

And in the afternoon of that far-away day, the solicitor had come up from Lepeton, and there had been the reading of the will, and David's embarrassment and guilt when they learned that all had been left to him – money as well as land, because a good farmer will never, if he can help it, separate the two. Well, he thought, I got it in the end.

'It's not your fault,' Ann said. 'You mustn't think it is.'

His mother had said: 'You don't feel badly about it, do you, darling? It doesn't mean that Grandfather didn't like you, you know. He was very fond of you. He told me all about this. He knew David wanted to be a farmer, and that you didn't. It means that all my money goes to you – all that your father left. You will be able to have the very best training an engineer could have. You do see that, don't you?'

He had said yes, more bewildered by his mother's seriousness than anything else. He had always expected that Blind Gill would go to David; neither property nor money counted for anything against his one overwhelming feeling of distaste, repugnance, for the fact and presence of his grandfather's death. Now that the funeral was over and the blinds had gone up again, he wanted only to forget that grimness and shadow.

'You will have quite enough, darling,' his mother had said. He had nodded impatiently, eager to be free of this conversation which was a last link with the unpleasantness of death. He took as little note of the urgency of his mother's tone as he had done of her increasing pallor and thinness in the past year. He did not know, as she did, that her own life had only a short time to run.

'Johnny,' Ann said. She came and put her hands on his shoulders. 'You must snap out of it.'

And after that, he thought, the holidays with aunts, and his comradeship with David, all the deeper for their shared isolation. Had there been, beneath all that, a resentment of what his brother had – a hatred concealed even from himself? He could not believe it, but the thought nagged him and would not be quieted.

'Everything's going to be all right,' Ann said. 'The children can grow up here in peace, even if the world is in ruins. Davey will farm the valley land.' She glanced at the body lying on the bed. 'David wanted that more than anything.'

John spoke then. 'He'll do more than farm it, won't he? He will own it. It's a nice bit of land. Not as much as Cain left to Enoch, though.'

'You mustn't talk like that. And it wasn't you who killed him – it was Pirrie.'

'Was it? I don't know. We'll blame Pirrie, shall we? And Pirrie is gone, washed away with the river, and so the land flows with milk and honey again, and with innocence. Is that all right?'

'John! It *was* Pirrie.'

He looked at her, 'Pirrie gave me his gun – he must have known, then, that he was finished. And when I saw that he had gone under, I thought of throwing it after him – that was the gun which brought us here to the valley, killing its way across England. I could have got to the shore more easily without it, and I was deadly tired. But I hung on to it.'

'You can still throw it away,' she said. 'You don't have to keep it.'

'No. Pirrie was right. You don't throw away a good weapon.' He looked at the rifle, resting against the dressing-table. 'It will be Davey's, when he is old enough.'

She shrank a little. 'No! He won't need it. It will be peace then.'

'Enoch was a man of peace,' John said. 'He lived in the city which his father built for him. But he kept his father's dagger in his belt.'

He went to the bed, bent down, and kissed his brother's face.

He had kissed another dead face only a few days before, but centuries lay between the two salutations. As he turned away towards the door, Ann asked:

'Where are you going?'

'There's a lot to do,' he said. 'A city to be built.'